Once Confronted

Once Confronted

Copyright © Lynne Stringer 2016
Published by Rhiza Press
www.rhizapress.com.au
PO Box 1519, Capalaba Qld 4157

National Library of Australia Cataloguing-in-Publication entry
Creator: Stringer, Lynne, author.
Title: Once confronted / Lynne Stringer.
ISBN: 9781925139785 (paperback)
Subjects: Interpersonal relations--Fiction.
Dewey Number: A823.4

All rights reserved. No part of this publication may be reproduced, stored in a retrieval system or transmitted in any form by any means without the prior permission of the copyright owner. Enquiries should be made to the publisher.

Once Confronted

Lynne Stringer

Also by Lynne Stringer

Veridon Trilogy:
The Heir
The Crown
The Reign

To the passers-by who helped me after my own 'incident'.

I don't know who you are, but thank you for what you did.

Chapter One

I could have been in Europe. But I wasn't. I was in Sydney.

I didn't have anything against Sydney, not really. It just hadn't been my ideal destination for my gap year.

It was too close to home, for a start. Home was Brisbane; only an hour or so away by plane. And *this* definitely hadn't been what I'd hoped for. How on earth had someone like me got a job in a bookstore?

Okay, so it wasn't just a bookstore. We had a café as well. That at least made it bearable but I still knew I wasn't the right person to advise our customers on the best book to buy. I didn't even like reading that much!

I was working from two until eleven and I tried not to drag my feet as I headed down the street. Newtown's shopping precinct was busy that afternoon. I could see staff plying their trades at the quaint stores and cafés around me. I should have got a job in one of them.

At least there was one good thing about working in Your Corner Bookstore and Café … well two, actually. For a start, we made pretty decent coffee. There was another bonus as well—Evan. As the thought of him came to mind, I checked myself out in the reflection of the shop window I was passing. My aqua shirt brought out my hazel eyes, as I had intended, and my blonde hair was sitting neatly. I brushed the bangs back from my face, arranging them just so.

The next shop was ours, and I walked through the doorway and up to the counter.

'Hi there, Maddy.'

I gave him my best smile. 'How's the day, Evan?'

Evan's bright blue eyes sparkled merrily as he handed a customer his flat white. 'Great. Just give me a sec and I'll make you one.'

'Do I look like I need it that bad?'

'No, but coffee makes any day brighter.'

He always said that, and I agreed.

As he handed me my drink, I glanced sideways at him. I wasn't sure what Evan thought of me. After all, I'd only met him a few weeks ago when I'd started work. He was twenty-five, seven years older than me, but I knew he was single and the looks he gave me made me wonder if he was thinking of asking me out. I hoped so.

I put my bag in the staff room area at the back of the store. It was a reasonable size, given how small our shop was, and had a place where we could sit quietly for lunch.

On my way back to the front of the shop, I looked at the bookshelves and sighed. I'd probably have to clean them again soon. The store's owner, Michael Overland, liked us to keep the books looking tidy. He'd squeezed as many shelves as he could into the store, even covering the two large glass windows at the front with them.

We had no front door as such, as Michael had told me he wanted people to smell the coffee as they walked past, and he'd moved the serving counter away from the door so they had to walk past a few shelves of books before they could order.

The shop also had little lighting, making it 'atmospheric', according to our boss. Ever since I'd started working there I'd wondered how any of the customers managed to read the books on the shelves. There were a couple of reading lamps set up by the tables around the room, but other than that, it was pretty dark. I'd often thought the dim lighting might be a marketing strategy. Maybe people wouldn't buy the books so quickly if they knew what was in them.

As I sipped my coffee, I noticed a new pile of books stacked near the staff room door. I groaned.

Evan followed my gaze. 'Yep. Sorry. A new delivery came yesterday.'

'I hoped you'd have done them all by now.'

He chuckled and put his hand on the unsteady pile. 'We ran out of time. It's been busy and Janice has been sick the past couple of days.'

'So she won't be in at all today?'

'Nope. It's just you and me until eleven.'

I turned to the pile and began sorting them into different genres. Why couldn't I have got a job in a fashion outlet?

My phone buzzed.

Off to bed after a great night out.

I frowned as I typed. *Isn't it six in the morning in Paris?*

Like I said, a great night out. Tell you more later. Wish you were here!

It wasn't fair. I shoved my phone back in my pocket violently.

Evan raised his eyebrows. 'Another text from your friend? What was her name again?'

'Crimson.'

He shook his head. 'She sure likes to gloat.'

'No, she wouldn't do that. She just wishes I was there with them. So do I.'

When my two school friends, Crimson and Elaine, had come up with the idea of going to Europe for our gap year, we were all ecstatic. It seemed like a fantastic adventure for all three of us. It had never occurred to me that my parents would say no.

But they had. My mother was a worrier, so it was out of the question. 'Madison, Europe is too far away,' she'd said. 'What happens if something goes wrong? Dad and I don't even have passports.'

'Then get one,' I'd growled.

My dad's eyes had flashed at me. 'That's enough with the attitude, Madison Craig. And your mother does have a valid point.'

He'd only backed down because he knew he'd never change

Mum's mind. My dad often joked that I got my eyes and my stubbornness from her and everything else came from him. She wasn't about to let me win.

Elaine had had no trouble getting her parents to agree. Her family was loaded. It had taken Crimson a little longer to convince her mum, but since her dad had agreed to pay, she said okay.

But my parents wouldn't budge.

Eventually, they'd agreed I could go away, but only as far as Sydney. So I was staying with my Aunt Myrtle. That was no fun, let me tell you. Admittedly, she let me pretty much do what I wanted and had helped me get this job, but she was a sixty-something-year-old hippie. I was on my own with just her to keep me company. Fantastic.

Meeting Evan on my first day of work had made things look up. The others at the bookstore weren't that interesting. Michael was in his thirties and was a divorcee with three kids, and all the other staff were older women. Evan was the store's saving grace.

He'd become chummy with me when he'd heard my tale of woe, and I'd shown him a few texts from Elaine and Crimson, who tried to keep me up to date with what they were doing so I didn't feel too left out.

'At least working here will give you some money for your first year at uni,' he said, as he prepared an order for another customer. 'Do you know what you'd like to study yet?'

'No idea.' I helped him with the order, taking care to ensure I did it right. I still wasn't used to making proper coffees. My only work experience prior to this had been at a fast food joint. Their coffee didn't compare.

'What are you interested in?'

That was the billion dollar question. 'Nothing, really. Well, nothing you can make a career out of.'

'Do your friends come to you for advice?'

'I don't know. Maybe. I know they like talking to me. They have things going on in their lives that I don't. Like my friend,

Crimson. Her parents are divorced. She still sees her dad but he tends to give her money rather than time, you know? She likes to debrief with us sometimes.'

He nodded.

'How about you?' I asked. 'You're here full time. You must really love coffee … and books.'

'I do. I also enjoy the atmosphere of a small store. I like small businesses and I like people and getting to know them. Michael's also an old friend of the family. He gave me my first job, which was here, part-time, while I studied bookkeeping. Then he took me back again when I lost my job as a bookkeeper last year.'

'So are you just working here until you can find somewhere else?'

'No, I like to interact with people. You don't get that as much with bookkeeping.'

I really liked Evan. Janice had told me during one of our shifts together that he'd had a girlfriend but they'd broken up when he'd lost his other job. That girl clearly wasn't the kind who was loyal, unlike me. Hopefully, Evan would see that difference in me and give us a go.

***

The day went quickly, mainly because we were constantly busy, with people in and out. I knew Michael would be pleased with how much we'd taken. I didn't have any time to put the new books away until we were nearly ready to close.

With eleven o'clock fast approaching, Evan gave the pile of books a pointed look. 'We need to get stuck into those, especially since things seem to have finally quietened down.'

'Do you think Michael will worry, given that we haven't put them away because we've been so busy?'

He cocked his head. 'That's certainly a plus, but you know that people are more likely to buy …'

'When they can find a book on the shelf,' I finished for him. That was Michael's favourite mantra.

I checked to see if there were any more customers coming in. Nope. I'd been cleaning the tables constantly throughout the day, so I only needed to give one or two a quick wipe and they were all good. Then I reluctantly turned to the books I'd sorted earlier.

I glanced at Evan, where he stood looking at the cash register. 'Maddy, I think we're out of cash register tape. I'm just going to grab some from out the back.'

He walked past me, dodging the piles of books I'd spread out on the floor, and ducked into the back room.

As he did, two men came into the store. One looked irritated, but the other leant all over the counter and grinned at me. 'Hi, love. Can we get some coffee?'

I walked over to the coffee machine. 'Sure. What would you like?'

The man at the counter smiled in a way that made me feel uncomfortable. His blue eyes gave me the once over. 'I think a cappuccino would be great.'

I tried to keep my smile in place, wishing Evan would hurry up. How long did it take to find cash register tape? I turned my attention to the other guy, who was younger and had his hair back in a ponytail. 'Anything for you?'

He started, as though he was surprised I was speaking to him. 'No, nothing.' Then, when his friend gave him a sharp look, he said, 'Actually, I'll have a decaf.'

Yeah, I think you need it.

As I grabbed some cups I felt a movement behind me. I turned, assuming one of the men was going to ask me a question. Then I froze.

There was a gun aimed directly at my face.

At first I thought it was a joke but that feeling only lasted for a split second. The older man kept the gun level with my eyes. 'Make a sound and you're dead.' His voice was low but there was no mistaking the menace in his tone. Those cold blue eyes were now focussed and hard.

The younger man came around the counter and grabbed me by the arm. He dragged me over to the cash register. 'Open it now and we won't hurt you.'

The other man stayed on the opposite side but the gun was still pointed straight at me.

I was so terrified I couldn't remember what to do at first, then my hands were shaking so much I struggled to do it. All that money from our great day's sales. Why hadn't I cleaned the cash register out earlier?

When I opened the drawer, I realised Evan had moved some money himself. He must have put some of the larger notes under the drawer. We often did that to keep it out of sight.

But the man with the cold blue eyes scowled as he looked at the contents. 'Where's the rest of it?'

I was about to squeak out a reply when Evan came around the corner. 'Sorry. It took me a while to find—'

Cold Eyes turned his gun on Evan. As if on cue, the younger guy who was still standing next to me produced his own weapon and put it to my head. He held my arm in a pincer-like grip. Every time he turned his head, his oily unwashed ponytail whacked me in the face. It reminded me of an oil slick.

'Don't try anything,' Cold Eyes said. Then he gestured with his gun. 'Come over here.'

Evan glanced at me and seemed relieved I was unharmed. I tried not to look too scared. He came over slowly, probably trying not to make any sudden moves, but the man didn't seem pleased with his pace and took his arm to hurry him along. 'We don't have all day. Where's the rest of it?'

Evan remained calm. 'That's it.'

'Don't mess with me, mate. Get it out *now* or my friend will shoot her.'

I felt the barrel of the gun press against my temple. I held my breath in terror.

That made Evan's shoulders slump. 'Just give me a second.'

His hands shook as he took out the contents of the drawer and put it in a bag the slick-haired guy held out for him. When it was empty, Evan looked at me before picking up the drawer and taking out the money he'd hidden underneath. He put it in the bag as well.

The man smirked. 'Too slow.' He snapped his arm back and pistol-whipped Evan on the side of the head. To my horror, Evan collapsed to the ground, where he lay unmoving.

I started to scream. 'Evan! Evan!' There was no response. What had Cold Eyes done? One punch could kill. What if he was dead?

Slick gestured at the door. 'Let's go.'

But Cold Eyes turned his gaze back to me. 'Maybe we should take her.' He dragged me around the counter to the door. I screamed with every step and tried to twist away from him.

Slick cursed at him and shoved me away. I landed on the ground with a thud, my back slamming against the doorway. 'Forget her. Let's get out of here!'

I held my breath, afraid they would fight, but Cold Eyes turned back to me. 'Thanks a lot, pretty girl.' He blew me a kiss.

I sat there sobbing, unable to do anything. We needed help. Why couldn't someone help us?

I looked around the doorway and saw a young couple walking down the street.

'Stop them!' I screamed. 'They've robbed us!'

My attackers had dived into their car, which they'd parked in the loading zone out front, and with a screech of tyres, they were gone. The two passers-by weren't in time to stop them but the man turned to his girl as they reached me. 'I've got the licence plate.'

She nodded. 'That's good. We need to call the police.' She turned to me. 'Are you all right?'

But I just screamed at them, 'Call an ambulance. It's Evan. I think he's dead!'

They followed me back into the store, where Evan was still lying slumped on the floor behind the counter.

The woman checked his pulse. 'His heart's still beating and it looks like he's breathing.' She pulled out her mobile and dialled emergency.

The guy looked at me. 'They'll want to know what happened.'

'What do you think happened? They robbed us! They threatened us with guns. They hit Evan.' I sank to the floor. 'They've got to find them.'

'You let the police worry about that. Just sit tight and we'll get some help for you and your friend.'

I smiled weakly at him, trying to calm myself, but the tears kept falling.

And my mother had thought it would be too dangerous in Europe! What I would have given to be there with Elaine and Crimson.

Chapter Two

I sat in the hospital waiting room, clenching my hands on the armrests, trying to stop them from trembling.

They'd brought both of us in. I'd insisted on going, making a fuss about the bruising I could feel on my back from when I'd hit the doorway after Slick had pushed me. I didn't think I needed any medical attention but there was no way they were going to leave me behind. I was too worried about Evan for that, even though he'd regained consciousness before the paramedics had arrived.

They'd taken him away somewhere once we'd reached the hospital, and even after the police had finished questioning me, I hadn't been able to find out anything about how he was.

The police called Michael Overland to tell him what had happened at his store, as well as Aunt Myrtle, who arrived at the hospital so quickly I wondered how many speeding fines she'd picked up on the way. She swept in and embraced me in one of her incense-laden hugs. For once, I didn't mind.

She held my face and looked intently into my eyes. 'Are you all right?'

I sighed. 'I'm fine. I'm worried about Evan.' I quickly explained what had happened to him.

She nodded when she heard he'd been conscious before he was brought in. 'That's a good sign. Hopefully it's just concussion or something like that.'

With that, she turned imperiously to the two officers who were still with me. 'This is my niece, who is in my care while she's in Sydney. Thank you, on behalf of her parents, for your fine work. I can see her home.'

They seemed amused by her. 'That's fine,' one of them said. 'I think we've got all we need for now.'

'Certainly.' She turned back to me. 'Maddy, I called your parents before I came. They wanted you to call as soon as I'd found you.'

I nodded as I reached for my phone to dial their number.

My mother answered on the first ring. She was beside herself. 'Oh, my darling! Are you all right? You must have been so scared. Dad and I will fly right down.'

'You don't need to do that.' As much as I wanted to see them, I couldn't have them flying down to Sydney just for me. Especially when I knew without a doubt that I was going straight home as soon as I could. I didn't want to stay in Sydney anymore.

'Of course we do, darling. We'll be there as soon as we can get on a flight.'

'Okay. Let us know when you arrive. We'll probably head back to Aunt Myrtle's soon.'

'Love you.'

Aunt Myrtle took my hand as I hung up. 'Shall we get going?'

I shook my head. 'I want to find out how Evan is first.'

'Maddy!'

I looked up at the sound of my name. Michael Overland had just arrived. He looked relieved when he saw me, the colour returning to his round face. 'Are you okay? They told me what happened.'

'I'm fine but Evan's not. They hit him. I'm not sure how he is.'

I started crying again and Michael put a tentative arm around me. 'Let me try and find out.'

But no matter how hard we tried, we couldn't find out much about Evan. 'I've called his parents,' Michael said. 'I think they've already come up.'

'I guess they probably did. I wouldn't know them if I saw them.'

'Never mind. I'll call them later and find out what's going on. Let's get you home.'

Aunt Myrtle put a hand on his arm. 'Michael, you do what you need to do. I'll take care of Maddy.'

He gave me a guilty look but nodded. 'Sure. That's probably for the best.'

'Call me as soon as you hear about how Evan is.'

'I will.'

Aunt Myrtle took me straight back to her federation semi. I was glad to see it, in spite of its dingy appearance. I'd found fault with every bit of it when I'd first moved in, but just then, even the glass bead drape across the back doorway was a wonderful sight.

We hadn't been home long when Michael phoned. 'Evan's going to be okay. They want to keep him for a bit but he'll be back to normal in no time.'

Relief washed over me. 'Thanks, Michael. That's great to hear.'

It was the early hours of the morning by then, but I didn't want to go to bed. I was afraid I'd have nightmares. Aunt Myrtle didn't seem to want to sleep either, so we kept each other company. She kept up a steady stream of her favourite herbal teas.

A few hours later, a taxi pulled up outside her place, and out climbed my parents. I had the door open before they reached it and flew into my mother's arms. 'Mum!'

Her hazel eyes mirrored mine and her hair, which usually framed her face in a soft wave of rich mahogany, was all over the place.

Dad put his arms around both of us. We were all crying. I'd never seen my dad cry before.

Mum pulled back and smoothed my hair. 'Are you all right, darling?'

I nodded. 'I think so.'

'Are you sure?' Dad asked.

'I'm fine.'

Mum started to cry again. 'Oh, Maddy, what you must have been through!'

Aunt Myrtle came out to join us. 'Yes, we're happy you're here, but let's not stand on the front doorstep and give the neighbours a show. Come on.'

Fresh cups of herbal tea were quickly on offer as my parents stowed what little they'd brought with them in Aunt Myrtle's craft room. Mum insisted on sitting close beside me on the lounge. At first I thought she was going to make me sit on her lap. Even Dad kept me within arm's reach. It was like they needed to touch me to be convinced I was really okay, and I didn't mind one bit.

Mum kept shaking her head. 'It must have been terrible.'

I sensed she wanted details but I didn't want to talk about it.

'At least they got the men,' she said.

I looked up. 'How do you know that?'

'It was on the news,' Dad said. 'We saw it at the airport.'

I couldn't look at him. I was afraid he'd see the fear in my eyes. 'The police caught them okay?'

He seemed reluctant to tell me. 'They got one of them.'

My heart went cold. 'One escaped?'

Mum shook her head. 'No, darling. The police chased them in their car until they crashed. One of them didn't seem to want to give in. He shot at the police. They had no choice.' She closed her eyes.

That had to be Cold Eyes. He wouldn't go down without a fight. 'He's dead?'

'Yes.' She looked distressed. I, however, felt my body relax a little for the first time since the robbery. I would never have to see those eyes again.

Talk began to flow around me. I let it. When my mobile started ringing, I wasn't sure I wanted to answer it, especially since it was from a number I didn't recognise.

Dad noticed my hesitation. 'Better get it, Maddy. It could be the police.'

I took the call. 'Hello?'

'Maddy?'

I sat up straight, recognising his voice. 'Evan? Where are you calling from? This isn't your number.'

'No, I can't find my mobile. I think it was left at … I think I lost it.'

I could see why it would have been left behind. 'Are you okay?'

'Yeah. Still in hospital, though. But they don't seem too concerned about me.'

'I'm so glad to hear that.'

There was an awkward silence on the phone for a minute. I was trying to think of something to say when Evan spoke first. 'Are *you* okay?'

'Yeah, I'm fine.'

'They didn't hurt you, did they? After I …'

'No, I'm all good. They checked me out and that was it.' I wasn't going to mention the bruises. They were nothing anyway.

I could hear his loud exhale at my words. 'Great to hear. Are you still with your aunt? I mean, you're not going straight back to Brisbane, are you?'

'I don't think I know what I'm doing yet.'

'Can I call you when I get out of here?'

'Sure.'

***

Mum and Dad stayed at Aunt Myrtle's federation semi with us for the next week. They went with me to the police station a few days later so I could give an official statement.

The police confirmed what Mum and Dad had seen on the news—Cold Eyes had been shot and killed.

'He drew his weapon on our officers and they were left with no choice,' one of them said.

They didn't need to justify it to me. I had no trouble imagining him coming out of the wrecked car, gun blazing. But I tried not to think about it too much.

As the week went on, Mum and Dad wanted me to go back to the bookstore, but I couldn't do it. It didn't stop everyone who worked there from coming around to see me, though.

Michael came a number of times. I'd never seen anyone look as apologetic as he did. At first he didn't say much about what had happened, except to check I was okay, but when he heard we were going back to Brisbane soon, he came for another visit, looking uncomfortable. Even Aunt Myrtle's herbal teas weren't enough to settle his nerves.

'I can't tell you how sorry I am all this has happened,' he said, running a hand through his short, jet-black hair. I could have sworn that some grey strands had appeared in the last few days.

Dad shook his head. 'Michael, this is hardly your fault. Shops are often the targets of thieves. There's nothing you could have done to prevent it.'

'Still, I can't help thinking that I shouldn't have let Madison work late so soon after she'd started to work with us.'

While I appreciated Michael's sympathy, I was getting frustrated. 'I think those guys would have been just as happy coming in the middle of the day if it would have worked better. They might be regretting that they didn't try that.' I looked down at my lap. 'Well, one of them's regretting it, anyway.'

Everyone went silent. I noticed that usually happened when I talked about the *incident*.

Michael started up again after the silence became awkward. 'I've been trying to figure out anything I can do or say to make this better, but I've got nothing. Well, not nothing. Would you like counselling, Maddy? They say it can really help after something like this. I'd be happy to pay for it.'

Mum smiled. 'We're going to look into it when we get home. We have a friend who knows someone. Thanks for the offer, though.'

'Anything Maddy needs.'

The doorbell rang, startling me. I tried to still my shaking hands so no one would see them.

'I'll get that.' Aunt Myrtle rose from her seat.

We sat quietly, Michael shooting guilty looks in my direction, while we waited for her to come back.

'Look who I found at the door,' came her cheerful voice after a few minutes.

We turned to see Evan making his way into the room. He looked tired and there was a bruise on the side of his head. I went over and gave him a hug. 'It's good to see you.'

He smiled. 'You too.'

As he held me, I started shaking again, my whole body this time, and then the tears started. He held me until I calmed down. When I stepped away from his embrace I noticed there were tears in his eyes too. In fact, Mum and Aunt Myrtle were crying as well.

Aunt Myrtle frowned as she wiped her tears away. 'Shouldn't you be at home resting?'

Evan sat down wearily in the chair my dad vacated for him. 'I heard you were leaving.' He looked straight at me. 'I couldn't let you go without saying goodbye.'

'I'm glad you didn't.'

Once he was seated, Aunt Myrtle filled a cup and put it in front of him. He regarded it with a smile. 'Aunt Myrtle's famous herbal tea? Maddy told me all about it.'

Aunt Myrtle gave me a suspicious look.

'Don't worry,' Evan added. 'She only said good things. It's been nice getting to know Maddy.'

As he looked at me over the rim of his cup, I could feel my face warming. I looked away, hoping no one would notice.

Michael saved me by changing the subject. 'I was just saying to Maddy that I'd be happy to pay for her to get some counselling after all this. I'd be happy to offer that to you too.'

He nodded. 'Thanks, Michael. We'll see.'

'Well, one thing we would like to say,' Dad said, 'is to thank you for sticking by Maddy in there. I know she appreciated you keeping your cool.'

Evan glanced at my father before lowering his head. 'No problem.'

I wanted to glare at my dad for embarrassing him but I was worried that would make Evan uncomfortable.

He stayed and chatted for a while, then said he needed to go. I had the sense he was growing annoyed. I was too. Michael didn't want to talk about anything other than what had happened. Personally, I would rather have talked about anything else.

I saw Evan to the door and stayed with him while he waited for his taxi to arrive. I was relieved to find that even Aunt Myrtle left us alone.

'When do you leave?'

'We fly out tomorrow morning.'

'I guess this is goodbye then.' He was quiet, looking down at his feet. Then he looked up. 'I was going to ask you out before all this happened. Would you have gone with me?'

'Sure!'

I think he was encouraged by my smile. 'You know, I've always wanted to visit Brisbane.'

'Well, now you have incentive.' I tentatively put my hand on his arm.

After a moment, he reached up and laid his hand over mine. 'I do. Can I call you?'

'Anytime.'

He glanced up at me again and I could see something else on his face. His eyes held an expression I'd seen in my own since the robbery. I usually called it helplessness. I wasn't sure if that's what it was.

'You know,' he said, and his voice was so low I wasn't sure I heard him correctly, 'Maddy, I'm really sorry.'

'About what?' What did he have to be sorry about? He'd done everything he could.

He looked down again. 'Nothing, I guess.'

As the taxi pulled up at the kerb, he raised his eyes to mine, then pulled me in for a hug. 'Text me when you get home so I know you're safe, okay?'

With that, he stepped out the door, waved and was gone.

It was difficult to watch him go. I'd liked Evan before but now we had a bond that had been forged in what we'd been through together.

I sighed as I shut the door and returned to the kitchen to listen to the talk flowing around me, as everyone gave their take on an event they would never really know anything about.

Chapter Three

I was relieved as the plane took off from Sydney airport and began its journey back home. Logically, I knew the city wasn't responsible for what I'd been through, but I was happy to be going back to boring Brisbane.

Crimes happen there as well, Maddy.

I tried not to listen to that pessimistic voice. Yes, crimes happened in Brisbane, but they'd never happened to me there before. Sydney had been tainted but my home city was still clean.

When we walked into our three-bedroom brick house I expected to feel at ease but it seemed like an alien environment. That unsettled me. I hurried down to my room, hoping things would feel more normal when I was there. I guess it did. Everything was still where I'd left it just a couple of months before. My bed had its floral doona on it, my desk was still in its place, and the board which I'd filled with pictures of Elaine, Crimson and me was right where I'd left it. I plopped my bag down on the bed and looked around.

It didn't feel like home anymore.

I looked at my phone. There weren't any new messages from the girls. They had been as supportive as they could be, considering they were still in Europe and in a different time zone.

Then I remembered Evan. I sent him a text. *Got home safely.* I put a smiley face after it.

'Maddy?' Mum came to the door. 'I took the liberty of ringing your old boss at Best Burgers. They're happy to have you back there if you want to go. Just give him a call and he'll let you know when your first shift is.'

I sighed. It seemed like going downhill to go back to working at a takeaway again, but it was probably a good way to get back into normal life.

'I also enquired about finding a counsellor for you. I've got a few phone numbers for you to call.'

I took the numbers from my mother and she smiled and left me.

My phone beeped. I had a text from Evan. *Good to hear. You'll be okay.*

I hoped he was right. I wanted to be okay again.

***

I held my head high the first day I left the house to go to work. The street was quiet as I walked up to the bus stop.

I'd spent the last few hours trading texts back and forth with Elaine and Crimson. They'd been upbeat, as usual. It was nice to have friends who were trying to make me smile. Mum and Dad seemed to be tiptoeing around me and only ever asked if I'd called the counsellors yet. I wanted to get some hours at work under my belt before I did that. Try and normalise things.

Back to the daily grind! I texted to Elaine as I walked. I knew that Crimson would be looking over her shoulder.

You'll do fine, sweets, she sent back. *You know the drill. There won't be any guns at Best Burgers.*

I sure hope not, I thought as I passed into the next street. It was a little busier there.

When I reached the corner, I stopped and waited for the lights to change so I could cross. As I did, some jerk in a muscle car screeched his brakes right beside me.

'Hey, sweetheart!' he called out the window.

My body flushed hot and cold and I was rooted to the spot.

I could only turn my head as he screamed down the street I'd just walked up.

I looked back at it, only now seeing the danger. It wasn't incredibly busy when it came to car traffic, but cars did go down it regularly. There were plenty of times a single car would slide past on the quiet street and there wasn't usually anyone else walking along.

What if Mr Jerk had gone down the street when I was walking down it by myself? What if he'd pulled over and dragged me into his car? No one would have noticed I was gone for at least an hour, possibly more if no one at Best Burgers bothered to find out why I didn't turn up for my shift.

So I could have been abducted by that man and no one would have known about it all day.

I managed to make myself walk to the other side of the road but I was shaking so much I wasn't sure it was a good idea to go to work after all. At least on this road there was more traffic. There were also other people at the bus stop. Plenty of witnesses. Nothing would happen to me there.

I felt like crying but managed to keep it in. I would go to work. I would have a normal day. My shift was late, so Dad was picking me up afterwards. That was a relief. If I was like this in broad daylight, what would I be like if I had to walk these streets after dark?

I knew I would do everything I could to make sure that never happened.

***

'Maddy? Phone for you!'

I was chilling in my room, or trying to, anyway. The regular walk to the bus stop had become a nightmare, as had every time I needed to go somewhere when there weren't many other people around. I had been trying to take my mind off it by looking at some uni courses for next year. My parents were prodding me gently to consider what I would do with my future.

My mother came down to my room with the landline. She handed it to me. 'I think it's the police.'

I felt like throwing up. I guessed I was about to find out if I'd need to go back to Sydney for a trial.

'Miss Craig?'

'Yes?'

'This is Detective Senior Constable Blake here. I was just getting back to you with an update on the court case. It seems we won't be requiring you to come down to testify.' I breathed a sigh of relief as he continued. 'The defendant is pleading guilty, so it won't be going any further.'

'Pleading guilty?'

'Yes. He's not denying the charges. It would be stupid for him to do that anyway. It seems he's going to plead that he was coerced into it by his companion. Unfortunately, judges do sometimes take those things into consideration, and that, combined with the fact that he has no criminal record, means that it's more than likely he'll get a lenient sentence.'

My heart sank. 'How lenient?'

'I'd think probably about five years or so.'

'And exactly how much time will he spend in jail?'

'He'll likely be eligible for parole in two or three years, I'd say, but he'll only get out if he doesn't cause any trouble inside.'

Two or three years and he'd be out. I wondered if Evan knew. At least I was up in Brisbane. I thought it was unlikely Slick would come looking for me. 'He doesn't have any record at all? I find that hard to believe.'

The officer chuckled. 'That doesn't mean he's never committed a crime before. It just means we've never caught him before.'

That wasn't exactly comforting.

'Don't worry about it. I know his kind. Even if he does get out in a couple of years, he'll probably do something else and he'll be straight back inside with a longer jail term.'

'That doesn't help his victims very much.' I couldn't keep the bitter edge out of my voice.

'I know and I wish it were different. There's not a lot we can do about it, though. Now, you've been put on the victims register, which means someone will keep you up to date with what's happening with him, but I wouldn't waste too many more thoughts on him. I doubt you'll ever see him again.'

Evan called me later that night and we commiserated with each other. 'I can't believe he'll spend so little time in jail.'

'I know,' he said. 'I've seen this kind of stuff on the news all the time, with people arguing about lenient sentences for criminals. It's really weird that I'm the one it's happened to.'

'It's so unfair.'

'It's all right, Maddy.' There was reassurance in his voice. 'You don't live around here so even when he does get out, I can't imagine you'll run into him.'

'Yeah, it's nice to think that I'm just that little bit further away from him. Doesn't stop me worrying, though. Doesn't stop Mum worrying either.' I'd told my parents earlier about what the police had said. They hadn't been impressed with the sentence.

'Well, if he decides to target you, he should be the one who's worried.'

'Why?'

'Because I'll break every bone in his body before I let him do anything to you.'

It made my heart warm to think that he would go to those lengths to protect me. 'That's nice to know.'

'With any luck, he'll come after me first. I mean, I'm a local. Then I can take him out before you even have to know about it.'

He sounded serious and I could understand that. I wouldn't mind some pain being done to that guy, even though it had been Cold Eyes who'd really creeped me out. But I wasn't sure I'd ever be capable of hurting someone, even a guy like that.

'How's Michael going?' I asked.

'He's fine. Sales have picked up. What happened seems to have given the shop a bit of notoriety. He isn't complaining.'

'Are you still working there?'

He sighed. 'No. I couldn't take it anymore. My brother's given me a job doing bookkeeping for his mechanics business. It pays the bills, but I'll see if I can get something better. How about you? Are you working at the fast food place again?'

'Yeah, but Mum and Dad want me to make a decision about university. Still not sure what I want to do, though.'

'Whatever you want to do you'll be great at it, Maddy. You really will.'

I could feel my face turning red and was glad he couldn't see it. 'Thanks.'

'Don't let what happened hold you back.'

I smiled. 'Any plans to visit Brisbane soon?'

He laughed softly into the phone. 'Maybe. Let me get myself established at my brother's first. You should see his books. They're a mess.'

'Okay. And I'll let you know what I decide about uni.'

I hung up the phone feeling just that little bit better. It was always nice talking to Evan. I didn't have to explain to him what I was going through. He understood it. He was living it himself.

It was difficult to deal with on a daily basis. The oddest things would scare me. Places that had never bothered me before were now terrifying, just like the walk to the bus stop. I found I usually relaxed in places where there were lots of people, although there were still times when even that would freak me out. I might see someone who reminded me of those two guys, particularly anyone with cold blue eyes, and I would start to shake and have to get away from them fast. It was hard when it happened at work. Sometimes I had trouble serving people just because they looked like one of them. Fortunately, I managed to hide it.

However, I had no hesitation in agreeing to go and pick up Elaine and Crimson from the airport when they came back from their overseas adventure. They were coming back after only five months away, having run out of money.

I was nervous as I walked into the terminal from the car park. I made sure I waited until there was more than one person around so I would have a witness if someone turned nasty. I tried not to think how twisted it was to worry about that.

The plane was late, as usual, but eventually I saw Elaine and Crimson stumbling towards me, looking half-asleep.

Crimson reached me first. She'd had her hair curled. It formed a mass of thick black ringlets around her head. She reached out for me and gave me a big hug. 'How are you doing, my lovely?'

I smiled. 'Fine, thanks.'

Elaine was only a few paces behind, her hair just as red and straight as ever. She seemed to have gained a few more freckles in spite of the fact that she'd been away from the Queensland sun.

'Hey there, darling,' she said, wrapping her arms around me. 'How's regular life going? No more holdups?'

I rolled my eyes. 'Don't mention that, please.'

'Why not?' Crimson said. 'It's a great story to tell. Your grandchildren will love it!'

'Not if they had to live through it.'

After we'd got their luggage, I led them back to the car and we packed it all in. It was a tight squeeze—my car wasn't that big—but we made it.

'Something tells me you've brought back more than you took with you,' I said as I settled behind the steering wheel.

Elaine grinned. 'You bet. We had to bring you back something, didn't we?'

I smiled. 'You mean it's all for me?'

Crimson thought about that. 'Maybe not all of it.'

I laughed. I'd had a feeling that would be the case.

'Have you decided what you're going to do at uni yet?' Elaine asked.

I nodded. 'Social work.'

Crimson's eyes lit up. 'Social work? Really? And where did that come from?'

I should have thought the answer to that was obvious. I gave her a look.

'Because of what those monsters did to you? Well, that's great.'

'Crimson,' Elaine cautioned.

'No, I'm serious. You're taking something bad and turning it into something good. Are you going to help other people like you?'

I raised my eyebrows. 'Like me?'

'You know, other victims.'

I flinched. I didn't like thinking of myself as a victim, even though it was true. She was also correct. That was exactly what I was planning to do. My parents had been delighted when I'd told them that I hoped to be able to help people who'd been the victims of violent crime.

'How are you going really?' Crimson asked. I'd expected the third degree from her.

I shrugged. 'Okay, I guess.' I hadn't told them about the difficulties I was having going anywhere. I hadn't wanted to worry them.

'How's counselling been going?' Elaine asked.

'Not bad.' My fortnightly counselling sessions had helped a bit, although I hadn't appreciated it when the counsellor had told me she didn't know how long it would take me to get better. It was different for everyone, apparently, but I wanted an exact date when things would be normal again.

'Some days it's difficult. You know, if I see someone who looks like one of them,' I said. 'It's scary when that happens.'

'Maybe you need to get out more.'

I rolled my eyes. I should have guessed that would be Crimson's solution for everything.

Elaine seemed to agree with me. 'Crimson!'

She looked back and forth between us. 'What? I think that would help. See as many people as possible. You know what they say—when you fall off a horse, you should get straight back on.'

'Not sure that really works in this case.'

'Of course it does!' she declared. 'You need to take the bull by the horns. What are you doing this Friday?'

'Nothing.'

'You are now. We'll go out.'

'Friday?' I said doubtfully.

'Yeah. You don't have any plans, do you? We need a couple of days to recover from the jetlag. Although maybe jetlag will make it easier to stay up all night.'

She grinned and I joined her. I'd missed the two of them. It was great to have them back. And maybe Crimson was right. Maybe I had been cowering too much. 'Friday it is.'

***

We caught a taxi into the Valley on Friday. I wasn't much of a drinker but I knew the other two were and I didn't want the responsibility of driving the two of them home if the evening went that way.

'Relax, sweets,' Crimson said when I told her that. 'This is all about you, after all.'

We settled into her favourite nightclub. Elaine spent most of the time pointing out any guy she thought might interest me. Crimson kept trying to find people who looked like my 'crims', as she called them.

'Look, there's a new one!' Elaine told us as a couple of guys came in. One was blonde. She loved men with blonde hair. 'I wonder if he's taken.'

When he and his friend glanced in our direction, she almost swooned. 'Look, they're coming over!'

I don't know if Crimson saw the panicked look on my face, but she asked, 'Do either of them look like … you know?'

I shrugged. Both of the men in the store that day had dark hair, much darker than either of these two.

'Hey girls,' the blonde one said. 'I'm James and this is Trevor.' His friend nodded. 'Would you like us to buy you a drink?'

'We're good at the moment, thanks,' Crimson said, pointing to our glasses, 'but you can join us.'

Both Trevor and James seemed like nice guys. They chatted casually to all three of us. They kept drinking, though, which made me nervous. My mother had always cautioned me about drunk men and what they could do. It was one warning from her I'd actually taken seriously and now it was more frightening than before.

Eventually, James took Elaine out on the floor to dance just after Crimson returned from getting another drink. I declined anything else and tried to hide my nerves.

'Stop that,' Crimson said to me when Trevor went to use the men's room.

'Stop what?'

She grabbed my hand, which was wrapped around my glass. 'That nervous tapping your fingers are doing.'

I pulled my hand away from my glass with a sigh. 'Sorry.'

She gave me a long look. 'You going okay?'

I shrugged. I didn't want to spoil their night.

She wasn't fooled. 'If you've had enough, say so and we'll go.'

I appreciated the offer but I wasn't big enough to call her on it. She was having fun. So was Elaine.

We could see Elaine from where we were. I wasn't sure she could see us, although she smiled in our direction every so often.

Crimson looked around for Trevor. 'He's taking his time.' She sighed. 'Maddy, I've really got to go myself. Will you be all right here for a second without me?'

I gulped. I knew it would take longer than a second in the ladies' room. But I could still see Elaine clearly. I didn't want to be the boring friend who spoiled everything, so I smiled at her. 'Sure.'

She put her hand on my arm and disappeared.

I don't know how long I sat alone but it must have been a good five minutes at least. I kept an eye on Elaine but she was being entertained by James and had stopped looking my way.

'Hello, beautiful.'

My heart lurched. The voice was slurry. I looked up to see a man leaning over me. His breath stank of beer. But more terrifying than that, in the pulsing light, I could see his eyes.

They were blue. Cold, icy blue.

I felt a shiver run down my spine but tried to play it cool. 'Hi.'

Without waiting for an invitation, he swung himself into the seat next to me. 'Anybody sitting here?'

I tried to stop my voice from shaking. 'Yes, actually—'

'Nah, they can find another seat.'

I jumped as I felt his hand on my thigh. I got up and moved away. He followed.

I could feel my breathing accelerating. I was going to lose it any minute. I was going to scream if he came any closer. His hand was in his pocket …

It was a gun. No, it was a knife. It was some sort of weapon, I was sure.

I was on the floor covering my head before I even knew what was happening. The sobs began to tear themselves from me. I curled into a ball. 'Please, don't hurt me, please …'

I wasn't sure exactly what happened next. All I remembered was seeing Elaine's panicked face next to mine. 'Maddy? Maddy? Are you all right? Did he touch you?'

She said it over and over again until I replied. 'I'm okay.'

I gradually uncurled and rose to my feet to see the man who had accosted me with a broken nose. I wasn't sure at first if Trevor had punched him or if it was Crimson. She was spewing venom at him while he tried to stem the flow of blood.

I was too out of it to notice much of what happened after

that. I remembered being asked if the guy had hurt me. I said no. I was worried they'd call the police if I said yes and I didn't want that. I didn't want to make another statement. Hell, I hoped I'd never see a cop again in my life. I didn't want there to be a reason to see one. Eventually, the cops did come and Trevor had to make a statement, as apparently he'd been the one to punch the guy out. They accepted my word though, when I said he hadn't hurt me. Elaine and Crimson told them about what had happened to me and they seemed to accept that that's what had made me freak out.

Eventually, the girls called a cab and we headed home. We were staying at Crimson's place that night and when we walked in I collapsed into the bed that had been set up for me and sobbed.

The girls waited until I'd calmed a bit before I felt Elaine's hand on my arm. 'I'm really sorry, Maddy. We shouldn't have taken you there. It was a bad idea.'

I felt terrible. I'd spoiled what should have been a good night for them. Crimson was pacing up and down. I wondered if there was anything I could do that would make this better.

'I'm sorry, guys,' I said, my voice breaking. 'I wanted it to be fun. I didn't mean to ruin it.'

I started crying again and Elaine patted my shoulder. 'You didn't ruin it, don't worry.'

'But you're seeing someone about this?' Crimson asked as she finally stopped pacing.

I sighed. 'Yeah, I've seen someone a couple of times. It all feels a bit strange though, you know? I mean, shouldn't I just be able to get over it?'

'Well, it was something that nearly killed you—' Crimson began before Elaine shushed her.

'I think we all need a good sleep,' she said softly. 'We'll go and have a nice breakfast somewhere in the morning. How about that? It will be all in broad daylight where everyone can see us. Then you won't be scared.'

I smiled to hide how bad I felt. I knew they were trying to help but what Elaine had said made me realise just how weak I was. Was this how it was going to be for me from now on? Forever looking for witnesses and afraid of blue-eyed men or men with ponytails? I had been carefree once. It seemed like so long ago now. Was that really gone forever?

I wasn't going to let that happen. I would get over it. Maybe going to uni would help. I hoped so.

Chapter Four

I shoved my bag underneath the desk and looked around. Good. I wasn't late. The room was still filling up with students.

It was my first month of lectures at university. I was doing a Bachelor of Social Work. It was at a relatively small campus and I'd worried at first that I'd be walking in lonely places by myself. That hadn't happened yet, though.

I'd been forced to take the bus as there was rarely any parking available. That was harrowing, especially if the session went late. However, my father, after speaking to my counsellor, had agreed that it was better to have someone pick me up if I had to come home late … at least at this stage. I was going to work on that and had been given a number of things to do to try to rebuild my confidence.

I'd been surprised by how many people studying this course weren't school leavers. Even as I looked around, the woman with short brown hair was sliding in a few seats away from me. I guessed she was in her forties. She glanced at me and I smiled. She smiled back but there was something behind her smile, as there always seemed to be with her. I'd noticed it ever since our first lecture together. She seemed to look right through me.

Our lecturer, Astrid Monahan, walked in. I wished I could say she was inspiring. I couldn't tell how old she was. Her hair was a bright shade of red … this week.

She looked at us over the rim of her owl-like glasses. 'All right then, everybody. Welcome to class. I hope you've all downloaded the powerpoint I put up on the course website.'

I nodded. I had it ready on my tablet. I sneaked a glance at the girl sitting in front of me. She was too busy scrolling through Facebook to have heard what our lecturer had said.

With one more look around the class, she began. 'Today we will be discussing more on Erikson's eight stages of development ...'

She rabbited on for a couple of hours. I was diligent in highlighting the most important points on my tablet. I wanted to do well in this course.

As I packed up my things at the end of the lecture, I looked at my watch. It would be dark outside. I checked my phone. No message from Dad. Hopefully he would be waiting outside for me.

As I went to leave, the brown-haired woman fell in step with me. 'There's no reason to be afraid, you know.'

I stopped, embarrassed she had worked it out. 'What makes you think that—'

She waved her hand at me. 'Don't bother. Come on, I'll walk you out.'

I was a little angry at her for hanging around. Even though I knew that the presence of even one more person increased my protection level considerably, I wasn't sure I wanted her company. She was a bit too 'in your face'.

'Melanie,' she said as we walked.

'What?'

'My name's Melanie. Melanie Harper. I guessed you weren't going to ask, so I thought I'd tell you.'

'Nice to meet you.' I tried to make the words sound sincere.

She smirked. 'Yes, I know. You're wondering what this interfering middle-aged hag is doing talking to you and how I knew you were frightened to come outside by yourself.'

I didn't bother to say anything, especially since it wasn't a question.

'Don't worry. I'm sure you'll soon have a bevy of friends ready to drive you home.' Her eyes slid sideways. 'Probably plenty of guys too.'

I sniffed. I wasn't ready for a guy yet. I didn't want him to have to deal with all my anxiety stuff.

Although I didn't say anything, Melanie nodded. 'It was a guy, then. Were you raped?'

That stopped me in my tracks. Unfortunately, I'd just walked out the door and had to step out of the way to avoid the other students still streaming out behind me. I was even more flustered by the time I turned to Melanie. 'I beg your pardon?'

She gave me a knowing look. 'You're exhibiting all the signs of recovery from recent trauma. I've been watching you these last couple of weeks and I see how nervous you get out here while you're waiting for your ride home. I've also seen how diligent you are.'

I bridled. 'Is there anything wrong with that?'

'It does seem a tad intense when you're concentrating as though your life depends on it.'

I couldn't think of anything to say at first. 'Is it such a bad thing to want to do well in this course?'

She shook her head. 'Not at all. But I know it's trauma. I can recognise all the signs.'

'How?' I grumbled, continuing my walk to the car park. 'Because you're some kind of natural counsellor?'

'No, because I remember what it was like when I was there.'

That stopped me again. I couldn't see Dad in the car park anyway. I turned to face her. 'What does that mean?'

'I'm the victim of violent crime as well, honey. I know it when I see it. You're jumping at shadows. You don't necessarily like to be with people but you don't like to be alone either. You know no one really understands what you're going through ... unless they've been there themselves.'

I gaped at her. 'What happened to you?'

She shrugged. 'I married a drunk. He started beating me. I put up with it for three years until the night he nearly strangled me to death. After that, I left.'

I could feel a morbid fascination sneaking over me. 'When was this?'

'Ten years ago. It's taken me a lot of time in recovery to get where I am now. Once I was in a good place, I realised I wanted to come here.' She gestured at the building behind us. 'See if I could help someone else.'

I raised an eyebrow. 'Were you planning on starting with me?'

She chuckled. 'No, but I could tell you needed help, even though you don't need to be afraid. You're armed.'

I frowned. 'Sorry?'

She looked at the bag hanging from my arm. 'That's a student bag, isn't it? You got it at O-week?'

Yes, I'd got my bag at our university orientation week. 'What about it?'

'Do you know how many secret compartments it's got?'

I lowered the bag from my shoulder and looked at it. 'I know it's got some.' For the first few days I'd kept opening up different areas and finding things like pens, pencils, notepads and toiletries.

She reached for the side of my bag. 'I guess you haven't found this one yet.'

She pulled up a flap to reveal a zip. My curiosity got the better of me and I reached for it. Inside, there was what looked like a small can of air freshener. 'What's this?'

'Let me show you.'

She took it from my hand and yanked on a plastic tab on it. Then she pressed the button on the top and the little can let out a loud shrieking noise. Everyone in the car park turned to stare.

Boy, it was loud! I put my hands over my ears. 'Can you turn it off?'

'Sure.' She released the switch and handed it back to me.

I looked at the little can.

'It's a personal alarm,' she explained. 'They give one to all the new students.'

I nodded. I'd heard of these but had been too embarrassed to get one myself. It made me feel better to know I might have a way to alert someone if I was in trouble. I smiled at her. 'Thanks.'

To my disappointment, my dad drove up. 'Here's my ride. I'll catch you later.'

She waved as I jumped in, but before Dad could drive off, I wound the window down. 'Are you okay to get to your car or the bus stop or whatever?' The crowd had cleared and the car park was getting quieter by the second.

She grinned. 'My car's right there.' She indicated a sedan a few spaces away. 'And I've got my own alarm. I'll be fine. Thanks.'

***

After that day, Melanie and I became good friends, although my other uni friends, who were my own age, always rolled their eyes when I told them I was going to have coffee with her. Melanie was like Evan. She understood.

'Did you pick up much in Astrid's lecture today?' she asked me one afternoon, as she raised her coffee cup to her lips.

We were in the café on campus and had just come from another lecture. Happily, now that seven weeks had passed, I thought I was making progress in Astrid's class, although she was still difficult to follow sometimes.

'Not sure I got much today.' I sighed. 'I like the tutorials better. I get more out of them.'

She nodded. 'I've noticed that you're a "hands-on" kind of person.'

'That, and they're usually led by people who haven't been doing this for too long.' They were run by postgraduate students. 'They seem to have a better grasp on where we're at.'

'Are you managing to keep up with your assignments?'

I sighed. 'So far.' I'd always hated assignments. Writing was definitely not my forté.

She looked at me over the rim of her coffee cup. 'Wait until we start our placements.'

My eyes lit up. Our placements, the practical side of our studies, would start in our third year. 'Actually, I'm looking forward to that. I can't wait for the chance to help real people.'

'Hm.' Melanie fiddled with her cup as she laid it back on the table.

'What?' It was clear she had something on her mind.

She looked up at me. 'Can I speak frankly?'

'Usually it's hard to stop you.'

She laughed. 'You've noticed that, have you?' Then she looked down, deliberating something, before her eyes came back to mine. 'I think you're barking up the wrong tree.'

'Sorry?'

'I don't think you should have a career trying to help victims of violent crime.'

My heart sank. 'Why not?'

'I think you're going to struggle when they start telling you their stories. You won't be able to stay disconnected.'

'I can be disconnected if I want to.' I hoped the attitude in my voice would hide my uncertainty. What if she were right? If I didn't do this, I didn't know what I was going to do.

Fortunately, she changed the subject. 'How's Evan?'

I blew out some air, relieved. 'He's good. He's coming up to Brisbane for a week soon.' Just thinking about him made me happier. It would be good to see him again. We talked on the phone and on Skype as often as we could.

She gave me a sly glance. 'Am I going to get to meet him?'

I frowned. I didn't know if I wanted to introduce Evan to her. She might be too intense for him. I'd already planned a couple of outings with Elaine and Crimson and Crimson's new boyfriend, and one with my other uni friends, but I hadn't thought of Melanie.

She must have seen the terror in my eyes because she nodded calmly. 'It's fine if I don't.' She grinned. 'Just make sure you give me all the details, okay?'

I smiled. 'Sure thing.'

***

I checked my hair and make-up in the mirror. Evan would arrive any minute.

He'd been in Brisbane all week and I'd made the most of every moment. Elaine and Crimson loved him and spent a lot of time elbowing me in the ribs and winking every time his back was turned. I'd been receiving texts from them constantly and wasn't surprised when another one came through.

It was Crimson. *Ready yet?*

Just about, I replied.

Have fun! She put a whole line of smiley faces with it.

I knew why she was excited. Evan and I were going out by ourselves. Most of the week we'd been with other people, although we were usually alone when he dropped me off and picked me up in his hire car. We'd also spent what I thought would be an excruciating evening having dinner with my parents, although it hadn't turned out too bad.

I heard a car pull into the driveway and I double-checked myself in the mirror again. I couldn't find anything wrong with what it was showing me but I was still smoothing everything down when my mum yelled, 'Honey! Evan's here!'

I grabbed my purse and headed out to join him.

Butterflies fluttered in my stomach when I saw him. Although he'd lost a bit of weight since I'd seen him in Sydney, it hadn't made him look gaunt. If anything, it had made him look streamlined. His hair was still a light golden colour and his eyes still deep and blue. His face split into a grin as he saw me. 'Hey there. Ready to go?'

'Yes, sure.'

Mum leant in to give me a kiss and took the opportunity to whisper in my ear. 'You be careful.'

I glared at her as I said goodbye. What I did on a date was none of her business.

He took me to a restaurant down by the river. It had a wonderful outlook, and since it was a nice night, we sat outside to eat. I was surprised to see how classy the place was. The prices made my jaw drop.

'Don't worry about that,' he said, taking in my shocked expression. 'I'm paying.'

'You don't have to do that,' I protested, even though I didn't mean a word of it. How many guys did that these days?

'So how's uni going?' he asked as we ate.

I grimaced. 'I hope it's going okay. Sometimes I wonder if I've done the right thing, doing this.'

'Why?'

'I don't know.' Melanie's words had stuck with me. 'I'm afraid I've gone in over my head. What if I can't cope with hearing everybody's problems? I still don't know if I can deal with my own.'

My hand shook as I reached for my glass. Evan must have noticed, because as I laid my hand back on the table, he covered it with his. 'Don't let that define you. If you do, you let them win.'

'Who?'

'The scumbags who did this to us. If you let this take over your life, they're going to beat us. We have to show them they don't control us. We have to win the game.'

I screwed up my nose. 'I don't consider it a game.'

'But they do. We can't let them win, Maddy.'

He spoke with such passion he started to convince me. I didn't want to be the person who let the bad guys win. But I only wanted my old life back. I wanted to be confident Maddy who could go out somewhere without counting witnesses. Sometimes I wondered if she was ever coming back. But one look into Evan's determined eyes made me sure she would.

After dinner we went for a walk along the riverbank. Even with Evan beside me, I was still checking around me and was happy it was reasonably busy where we were walking. I could see him looking around too. It was clear he was trying to walk apart from the crowd but stay within their sight.

He caught me watching him and looked ashamed. I didn't want him to feel bad about it. I held his hand tighter. 'You know, it scares me, walking like this.'

I heard him make a noise in the back of his throat but he said nothing.

'Do you constantly keep an eye on who's around you?' I pressed.

His haunted eyes turned out to the river. 'Don't you think I can protect you?'

I hesitated and he shook his head. 'Don't answer that. You don't need to. I already know the answer.'

'Evan, it's all right. I …' What could I say? I knew his presence was no guarantee of safety, although it was more secure than if I were with another girl. And it was no reflection on him. It would be the same if I were with my dad.

He stepped towards the railing and looked out over the river. I wrapped my arms around him and eventually he turned and held me. We stood there for a while, ignoring the people around us.

His hand touched my cheek and he turned my face to his. His eyes were no longer haunted. They were soft and caring. 'Do you know how special you are?'

Without waiting for a reply, he covered my mouth with his. It was not the first time we'd kissed, but up until this point, it had just been a kiss goodnight. I sensed there was more behind this one.

As his mouth continued to explore mine, he held my face to his, stroking my cheek with his thumb. His other hand slipped up under my jacket and pulled me closer to him. I didn't resist. I was enjoying this. I felt something was rising in us both, something like expectation.

Passion was overriding everything. He held me closer, his hand slipping under my blouse and gripping the skin of my waist. I didn't want to hold back, but then I remembered I'd only been seeing him for a week.

He must have sensed my hesitation. 'I'm going back to Sydney tomorrow,' he said. I could see the pleading in his eyes.

Oddly enough, his words had the opposite effect to the one I thought he intended. I was sure he wanted me to go back to his hotel room with him, but I didn't want to feel pressured. I pulled away. I saw his frustration but he didn't push any further.

When he dropped me home there was more kissing and a plea to continue the night somewhere else, but Mum was already watching from the window. That was a temptation to change my mind, if only to remind her I was an adult, but I said goodbye to Evan and he promised to come back soon.

'I'd be happy to see you anytime,' I said with a smile. 'Call me when you get home.'

He nodded. 'Okay. I'll come see you again as soon as I can.'

One more passion-riddled kiss and I managed to leave the car and wobble towards the house.

Once I was inside I ignored my mum, who darted back into the living room so she wouldn't be caught snooping. I went to my room and pulled out my phone.

I'm back, I sent to Elaine.

That's early, she sent back. *Everything okay?*

Yep.

Want to talk about it?

Nope.

So why did you pick up the phone?

Couldn't answer that one. I sent her a flippant reply and turned off my phone. Then I tried to sort out what I was feeling.

What did I think of Evan? I wasn't sure. There was no doubt we had plenty in common. Well, we had one thing in common—we'd been through something terrible together. No one knew how I felt better than him. Even Melanie wasn't that good. And talking to her about my problems always made me feel guilty because she'd endured that terror for years and mine had only been for a few minutes.

Evan was the best at knowing exactly how everything affected me. He was a nice guy, caring, good-looking. What was there to dislike?

I didn't know. There was something niggling in the back of my mind but I couldn't put my finger on it. Had it been all that talk about winning? Was it really a good idea to see it that way? I knew from my own counselling sessions and what I'd learned at uni so far, that Evan's counsellor would have probably encouraged him to get past it with whatever he or she felt was a healthy coping mechanism for him. Maybe they'd realised he was competitive and thought that was the best way for him to overcome what had happened. My counsellor had been encouraging when I'd told her I was thinking of studying social work and she'd helped me work through the different ways my traumatic experience might impact my studies. So Evan's way of coping wasn't necessarily wrong. It just meant it was wrong for me.

Still, something about it disturbed me, but I tried to put it out of my mind. After all, it was a process. Evan was working his way through it, the same as I was. He was just going a different way from me.

Chapter Five

In spite of Mel's doubts about me continuing in my course, I felt confident as I started my second year of study. The first day back did nothing to change that feeling.

I didn't see Mel until later when I noticed her sitting outside with a group of students. They were all listening in rapt attention to a girl who I'd seen around. She wasn't much older than me and I was pretty sure her name was Lisa.

Mel waved me over. As I sat down with them, she leant over and whispered in my ear. 'Listen to this.'

One of my fellow students, a guy named Eric, was questioning Lisa. 'So how did you find out about this?'

'My counsellor told me about it. I wasn't sure it was a great idea at first, but after I'd talked to the people involved I started to think it might help.'

Another girl, Rachel, jumped in. 'And did you tell him what you thought of him?' She raised her fists as if she wanted to punch someone.

Lisa gave a nervous laugh. 'I thought I was going to, and I did yell at him once, but he seemed so sorry. It was difficult to stay mad. After all, he was just a stupid kid.'

Eric snorted. 'That's no excuse.'

I frowned and leant over to whisper to Mel. 'What happened?'

Unfortunately, replying softly to me wasn't Mel's style. She turned to the group. 'Can you fill Maddy in on what happened, Lisa?'

Lisa looked back at me and paused for a moment to pull her ponytail tighter. 'Yeah. I was just telling the others about something I did on the holidays. It's called a restoration conference. It's when someone, a criminal, commits a crime against you, and you meet with them to talk it out.'

I felt a cold feeling creep over me. 'What happened to you?'

'Last year I was mugged. A guy with a knife came up to me and took my wallet. It really shook me up. It only lasted for about thirty seconds. I couldn't believe how much it affected me.'

'And you agreed to see this guy?' I tried to keep the incredulity out of my voice.

I think she still picked up on it anyway. 'Yeah. I mean, I didn't think I would at first. But everyone I spoke to said it would help me move on.'

'Yeah, especially if you get to tell him what you think of him,' Rachel put in.

Lisa smiled. 'I thought that at first too, but when I met him, he was so young. He did it to impress his friends. And he was sorry, especially when I told him how scared I still was. I couldn't stay mad at him after that.'

Eric scoffed at that, and the others continued asking questions, but I drifted off into my own thoughts.

Why would anyone want to meet with someone who'd done something like that to them? Was it really as beneficial as she said? But then, maybe it would help someone like Lisa, who'd only been through a thirty second ordeal. Mine had lasted longer than that, and Evan had been badly injured. Not to mention Cold Eyes trying to drag me away and Slick pushing me to the floor. I doubted they'd even suggest it for someone like me.

But when I noticed the expression on Mel's face I knew what she was going to say. No chance in hell.

Sure enough, she started as soon as the group broke up. 'That restoration conference thing sounds like a fantastic idea.'

'Yeah, maybe for someone like Lisa. Not for me.'

'Why?'

'Because mine was a lot worse than hers. It's not the same.'

Mel frowned. 'It's not that different. She was attacked. She had her confidence and security shattered, just like you did. Just because it happened more quickly for her than it did for you is completely irrelevant.'

I could feel my anger mounting. 'Oh, doesn't it? And would you do it with your ex-husband?'

What I'd said was a low blow but she didn't bat an eyelid. 'In a heartbeat.'

It looked like she was telling the truth, but I was sure when push came to shove, it would be a different matter. 'Well, why don't you go and do it then, Mel? Let me know how it goes, and then you can talk to me about doing it myself.'

I tried to keep my voice casual, but fear was gripping my heart. I was sure she would do just that.

***

Mel didn't mention it over the next few weeks, but she broke her silence one day when we were driving to uni. 'Have you thought any more about that restoration conference?'

I pursed my lips. 'Have you had yours yet?'

She scowled. 'No. There are a number of reasons for that, the main one being that my ex would never agree to it.'

'Then I'm sure *he* would either.'

'You never know. He might be up for it.'

I pinched the bridge of my nose. 'Mel, I don't want to meet with him. I'll be happier if I never see him again.'

'I'm not so sure about that.'

'*I* am.'

She said nothing else until we parked the car. Then she turned to me. 'Don't be mad.'

That was a bad sign. 'What?'

She took a piece of paper out of her bag. 'I looked into it for you.' She held her hand up when she saw my mouth open. 'Just wait a minute. Let me explain. I knew you wouldn't do it so I thought I'd ask some questions on your behalf so you can make an informed decision.'

We were walking across the car park, but fortunately, there was no one nearby. No one at uni knew what had happened to me and I wanted to keep it that way.

'One thing that should relieve you is that they won't even consider doing it until the offender's out of prison. Although, from what I hear, that's likely to be next year.'

'How do you know all this?'

She smirked. 'I have friends in the know. The great part is that they put me in touch with the prison chaplain. Apparently, he's the one who organises these things. So I wrote to him to see what he could tell me. Would you like to hear what he said?'

'No.'

She rolled her eyes. 'Come on, Maddy. This isn't an ironclad agreement. It's only something to consider.'

I huffed. 'Fine.' She was going to read it anyway.

'Great. Here it is.

'Dear Ms Harper,

'Thanks so much for your interest in restoration conferences. It's something that more and more people are taking up these days and has proved a great help to many.

'However, since the conference isn't for you, it's not something you should be organising. If Madison Craig wants to have one, she'll need to go through the Department of Corrective Services to organise it and it's a decision she needs to make.

'Not only that, it would not even be advisable to organise one until Jeremy Stannem is out of prison. I'm confident he'll be released when he's up for parole next year, as he's a model prisoner and someone who, I believe, has changed. He's spoken to me about what happened quite a bit, and I think he would be interested in pursuing this if it's something Miss Craig is able to do.

'However, I stress again, it needs to be her decision. If you want to share this information with her, feel free, and tell her I'd love to hear from her when she's ready, although, as I said earlier, these arrangements would initially need to be made through the Department of Corrective Services.

'Thanks again for your interest. Yours sincerely, Matt Pearson.'

I felt sick. The only good thing about the letter was that the chaplain confirmed it couldn't happen yet and it was my decision to make. But the rest of it ... A *model* prisoner? Really? Could the chaplain tell? Probably not. After all, this *Mr* Stannem would be on his best behaviour for someone like that. And did he really think I would go to Sydney (he sure as hell wasn't coming up here), pat his hand and tell him what he did to Evan and me was just fine?

I could feel tears coming to my eyes and Mel put a hand on my arm. 'I'm sorry, Maddy. I just want you to consider it. I think it will help. It could be the thing that helps you over the line in your studies too.'

'Don't you dare try and tell me this is about my degree.'

'It's not. It's about you moving on with your life and being free of your fear of him.'

That sounded appealing but I wasn't sure this conference would result in that. 'What if the opposite happens? What if seeing him makes me worse?'

'I don't think so.'

'And how would you know?'

She had no answer for that and I stormed off to my class. I had trouble concentrating all day, and by the time I got home I was wound so tightly I could hardly think straight.

I took some deep breaths and managed to settle myself down

before I faced my parents so they wouldn't see I was upset. I didn't want them to know about this restoration conference. What if they wanted me to do it? That wasn't going to happen.

***

A few days later I made the mistake of mentioning it to Evan.

He was furious. 'You're telling me that Mel contacted this chaplain person? I hope you're going to report her. That has to be illegal.'

'No, she just made enquiries.'

'What kind of a friend is she that she would do something like that? I hope you told her never to mention it again. And get her to tell the chaplain you're definitely not interested. You don't want to be in touch with that kind of idiot.'

'Who, the chaplain? He's just doing his job.'

'You know what these religious people are like. All they need is for someone to "see the light" or say they do anyway, and they'll think they've changed and that they are going to become some upstanding member of the community. This kind of thing happens all the time.'

I frowned. Even though I'd been thinking along a similar line initially, I liked to think that people could change, regardless of circumstance. 'Are you saying that a criminal can't turn over a new leaf?'

'Of course not. Do you know the statistics of how many guys who get out of jail just do something worse and then go straight back in? There's no such thing as rehabilitation. It's a myth. They're in there to keep them off the streets and away from decent people.'

'Why would the government go to all that trouble to try and rehabilitate people if it never worked? It must work some of the time.'

'Don't you believe it. They only keep them alive because no one's got the guts to pass legislation that's going to allow the death penalty again. They should bring it back. I'd support it.'

Did he really think that was a good idea, and for everyone,

even someone like a petty thief, a kid who'd committed a crime? 'You can't be serious. Not for all criminals.'

'I don't think there's any other solution, especially if you've got gullible idiots like this guy trying to convince the authorities they've been rehabilitated.'

'Let's just forget about it.'

'No way. We need to do something or I guarantee you this guy will keep hounding you. Make sure Mel tells him never to contact you again.'

I cringed. 'I don't think I need to do that.'

'Get his address from Mel and I'll write back.'

That was definitely not a good idea. 'No, it's all right. Come *on*, Evan!'

I could hear his sigh. 'Yeah, you're probably right. I just wish … damn it, I don't want you to have to deal with this.'

I smiled. 'I know. It's hard to have something like this bring it all up again.'

He was silent for a moment. 'You still find it hard?'

'Sure. Don't you?'

'Yeah. It's just that …' I could hear the hesitation in his voice. 'You seemed to be coping pretty well when I was up in Brisbane.'

I chuckled. 'Looks can be deceiving.'

'I guess.' He sounded thoughtful.

'Most of the time I'm okay, it's just when something like this happens that it all comes back.'

'Well, we need to make sure it doesn't happen again.'

After that I changed the subject. I didn't want to contact anybody, and I certainly didn't want to mention it to Mel again. I was hoping that if I ignored it, she would lose interest. And while she mentioned it a lot at first, it was less and less as the days passed.

By the time we were finishing up the year she seemed to have forgotten about it. I hoped so.

Chapter Six

Was I nervous? Yes, I was.

Now in my third year of studies, I'd started my placement. I was working in a domestic violence unit.

Melanie had commiserated with me when she'd heard I was there. 'At least talking to me might have given you some idea of what to expect.'

'So I'll hear a lot of women criticising men?'

She laughed. 'You'll probably hear plenty defend them too. It can be difficult to slip out from under their control and realise just how evil they can be.'

'I'm surprised they didn't give you this one.'

'They know my history. They're worried it will shake me up too much.'

I wondered why. From what I'd seen of Mel she seemed unflappable.

Then she narrowed her eyes at me. 'Do they know your history?'

I tossed my head. 'I don't have a history. I'm here because I want to learn to be a social worker.'

'Whatever.'

Her doubts echoed in my mind as I looked over at Elsa, my supervisor. She was a tall, blonde woman with an expressionless face. Her eyes were on me now as I tried to look confident while following her into the counselling room.

I ran through the list of things I had to remember. I should not be judgemental. I had to make it clear I believed what they were saying. I had to make them feel safe and offer them choices so they would feel they were regaining control of their lives.

Actually, I wouldn't be doing any of those things. I wasn't allowed to yet. One glance at Elsa had told me she wasn't one for breaking the rules.

She raised her eyebrows at me as we walked. 'This is a new client. I always prefer to bring students in with new clients rather than ones we already have a rapport with. I've checked with her and she's fine with you sitting in on this session.'

Elsa reached the door of the counselling room and put her hand on the knob. 'Remember, that's why you're here. You're sitting in only. You're not doing the counselling at this stage. That's my job.'

She opened the door and we entered the room. It wasn't large and the walls were painted blue. There was a little table in the middle with a glass of water on it, but little else. There were three chairs; one on the far side and two closer to us.

In the chair on the other side of the table sat Grace. She didn't look much older than me, possibly in her mid-twenties. Her eyes were cast down and hidden by a brown ridge of hair that flopped over them. Her clothes were old but clean and I couldn't see any injuries on her, not that that meant anything. Abuse wasn't just about physical violence.

Her eyes flicked up as the two of us took our seats and she smoothed down her clothes but said nothing.

Elsa put on a professional smile. 'Grace, thanks for coming in today. Talking to a social worker like this can be difficult. This is Madison. I told you that she would be sitting in on our session. Is that still okay? If it's not, just say the word and she'll leave.'

I knew that Elsa was trying to empower Grace by giving her the choice but she made me feel like an intruder.

Grace's eyes darted to mine. 'Yeah, that's fine.'

'Now, you're in charge of what happens in this space. Whatever you want or don't want to talk about is fine. I believe you've been staying in the women's refuge for a few days now? How are you finding that?'

'It's fine, I guess. I mean, they're really nice there.'

'Did they talk to you about safety items?'

'Yes, they checked my phone, changed my number and all my passwords and that kind of stuff.'

'Good. Now, when we spoke on the phone you mentioned you were referred to us by your local hospital. You said then that you would be happy talking to us. Is that still okay?'

Grace flinched. 'My husband doesn't know I'm here, does he? He wouldn't like me doing this.' Tears began to drip from her eyes. 'He'll kill me if he finds out. Maybe I shouldn't be talking about this.'

She jumped up, a panicked look on her face. I nearly leaped up to stop her, but Elsa remained calm. 'Grace, you're safe in this space. You don't need to talk to us if you don't want to. It's your choice, but I'm here to listen to you if you do want to talk.'

Grace resumed her seat hesitantly. I was relieved. I noted down what Elsa had said. She was good at her job. I hoped that when I had her experience that kind of statement would just flow.

I kept taking notes, trying to follow where Elsa was leading Grace. She eventually managed to get her talking about what her husband had done to her. I tried to plot how she'd done it.

I turned my attention back to what Grace was saying. 'I always did what he said. Always. But I didn't do it right and I guess that was the problem.'

'It sounds like he was very controlling of your behaviours.'

Her shoulders slumped. 'It's no biggie, since I didn't even seem to get dinner right. It was always too hot or too cold no matter how much I tried to make it just how he liked it. He didn't like the way I did the ironing and—' she stopped and swallowed. 'He'd correct me for that.'

I'd already noticed that she called it 'correcting' when she was talking about her husband abusing her.

'When you saying correcting …?' Elsa prompted.

'With the iron,' she replied.

I thought my eyes were going to fall out of their sockets. Elsa shot me a look and I tried to control my expression.

'That's not correcting, Grace. That's abuse and violence. There's nothing you have done or can ever do that will make you responsible for that happening to you.'

Grace rolled up her sleeves. There were old burn scars all over her arms. 'It was so hard to get it right.'

I felt faint. I tried to pull myself together.

'What else did he do, Grace?'

She sniffed back the tears. 'Well, he seemed to like sex … sometimes. Sometimes he didn't. I didn't even do that right.'

She lifted her confused face to ours. 'But even when he seemed to be enjoying it I still hurt.'

'In what way?'

She described some sexual abuse that was so horrible I tried my best to block it out. I felt like throwing up.

'So he raped you?' Elsa asked calmly.

She frowned. 'No. He's my husband. He can't do that to me.'

'What you just described was rape, Grace, not consensual sex between two adult partners.'

'But he always seemed so happy when we were doing it. He seemed to like me then too.' There was a strange light of happiness in her eyes. 'He'd look at me and say, "you're such a pretty girl". He'd say that all the time—'

I was on my feet and out of the room before I'd even realised I'd moved. I shut the door behind me and leant against the wall beside it, taking deep breaths.

In those two words Grace had taken me back to the worst day of my life.

Pretty girl.

He'd said that to me. I could feel the fear rising up within me as if it would choke me. All the things Grace had said about the abuse she had suffered came straight back to me, except this time I could see me going through it, abused by *him.*

I closed my eyes, hoping it would drive the images out of my head. It didn't help.

Elsa came out of the room. 'Are you all right?'

I tried to gather some professionalism around me but I was shaking and I could tell she noticed. 'I'm fine.'

She didn't look convinced. 'If you can't deal with it that's okay. Do you need a debrief? I can get one of the others—'

'No, I'm okay.'

I made a move to go back into the room and Elsa stopped me. 'This is difficult enough for her as it is. If you're going to crack, you're of no use in there. You'll only make it worse for her.'

The client had to come first. I understood that. 'Okay. I'll just sit out here for a bit.'

'Do you need a debrief?' She sounded irritated at having to repeat her question. She obviously wasn't going to let it go.

I got angry at her insistence. 'I'm fine.'

'I'll get Angela to talk to you.'

Angela wasn't as pushy as Elsa. She was a motherly type with a big figure and she hugged a lot. Fortunately, I was able to convince her I'd just had difficulty dealing with the level of abuse.

She nodded understandingly. 'A lot of students struggle with that. Don't take it to heart. It can be difficult to hear those things at first. You'll get used to it.'

That didn't make me feel any better. What did she mean? That I'd soon grow so used to hearing everyone's horror stories that I'd stop caring? Or was it that I now had a benchmark? Next time, I could say to myself, 'Well, this one's story isn't as bad as poor old Grace.' Was that a good thing?

Angela gave me lots of hugs and a cup of tea and by the end of the day, I think I'd fooled her into thinking I was okay. But then, maybe not. She was a trained social worker. Could I ever fool someone like that?

On my way home, I reminded myself that it was the first week. Things might get better. I would be helping people. I would see them succeed and make it through the hard stuff. Surely that would make it all worthwhile? There would be success stories.

Dad was reading something on his kindle when I came home. He frowned when he caught sight of my face. 'Hard day, honey?'

'Yeah.' I sat next to him and put my head on his shoulder. He put his arm around me. We used to sit like this all the time when I was younger. It felt good to do it again.

'Want to talk about it?'

I could feel the tears building. 'What if I'm no good at this, Dad?'

He chuckled. 'I don't think you can tell that from the first day of your placement. What you're doing is difficult. It'll take a while to get used to it, probably longer than most other jobs. But it will be worthwhile in the end. Most things that are worthwhile are difficult.'

'Yeah, but I cracked up in my first counselling session today.'

'I'm sure you're not the first student to do that.'

So I'd been told. It didn't make it any easier to deal with. 'But what if it doesn't work out?'

'Then it doesn't work out. Learn from the experience and see if there's something else you'd like to do that suits you better. But don't give up on this too soon, Maddy. I know it's hard, but if you really want to do this, you need to stick it out. You'll be glad you did.'

It was the last thing he said that stuck in my mind. Did I really want to do this? What if becoming a social worker was only some kind of knee-jerk reaction, an attempt to try and find some good from something horrible?

***

'So Mr Wonderful is coming up again in a few weeks, is he?' Crimson said from where she was sitting by my bed, painting her nails.

'Yes, Evan will be back next week.'

'For how long?' Elaine asked, giving me a coy look over the magazine she was reading.

'Just for a week.'

Crimson put the lid back on her bottle of nail varnish. 'You've got to get him to stay longer than that.'

I shrugged, but didn't answer.

'How's the study going?' Elaine asked.

'Good.' The girls didn't know how tough I was finding my placement. It was hard to hear everyone's terrible stories and see their struggles afterwards, especially since it was often two steps forward and six hundred steps back. I'd known before I'd started my placement that many women went back to their abusive relationships at least once but it was hard to watch it happen.

'That's our girl,' Elaine said, putting her arm around me. 'Saving the world and helping those who can't help themselves.'

Crimson rolled her eyes. 'You're such a drama queen.'

Elaine slapped her with her rolled up magazine. 'You can talk.'

I decided to deflect the conversation. 'How about you girls? How's your study going?'

'I'll be done at the end of the year,' Crimson said with satisfaction. 'Then I've just got to find a job.'

'Are there any jobs around for journalists these days with everyone writing online?' Elaine asked.

'That's why I've already given myself an online presence. You've seen my articles.'

Yes, we had. Crimson was constantly sending us links to pieces she'd written on every subject imaginable. I tried to like and share as many as I could.

'I'm trying to build a platform,' she continued. 'That should show the big guys I'm an asset.'

'How about your degree, Elaine?' I asked.

'One more year to go, just like you.'

Crimson wrinkled her nose. 'Why you want to go back to school I've no idea. Have you forgotten what we used to say about the teachers?'

'Teaching is a noble profession. Besides, I'll be a cool teacher.'

Crimson sniffed. 'There's no such thing.'

'Anyway, you'll have to tell us if anything happens with Evan,' Elaine said.

I cringed. My deflection hadn't worked.

Crimson gave me a speculative look. 'Do you think anything will happen?'

I sighed. 'I don't know. I'm not sure what I even want to happen. I mean, he lives in Sydney. I live in Brisbane.'

'So? One of you could move.'

'He doesn't seem to want to do that. He never mentions it, anyway.'

Elaine looked at me. 'What about you? Would you move down there?'

'I don't know.'

'I think you should.' Crimson put her arm around me. 'We have to give this story a happy ending. The knight in shining armour wins the girl of his dreams after defeating the big, bad monster and they live happily ever after.'

I tried to smile but I knew this wasn't some fairy story where the good guy killed the dragon and it was all okay. One of the dragons was still very much alive.

'So if you're done with us talking about your not-quite-love life, Maddy, maybe we can talk about mine,' Crimson went on.

Elaine rolled her eyes. 'Who is it this time?'

'I met a guy named Max last week.'

I exchanged glances with Elaine. Crimson seemed to consider it her duty to date every guy she met. We knew we would be there for a while listening to her, so I tried to stop thinking about Evan, my placement and the dragon that kept haunting me. And I wasn't sure just then if the dragon was Jeremy Stannem or Mel.

Unfortunately, Mel hadn't left things alone. She'd recently revealed she was still in touch with the chaplain and he seemed happy to answer her emails. She usually forwarded them to me, encouraging me to read them.

After the girls had gone, I noticed there was another one from her. I didn't know why I kept reading them, but I did, every time.

> Dear Ms Harper,
>
> Thanks for your continued interest in my work. I must confess your correspondence is something I look forward to. From the sounds of it, you've had a rough life, but you're doing your best to move forward. I hope you can eventually achieve peace after all you've been through.
>
> To answer your question, yes, Jeremy is now out on parole—

I stopped reading. I'd heard through the victims register that he'd been released. I'd been trying not to think about it too much. Although I was far from believing he would come after me when he got out, it played on my mind.

Evan had been furious when he'd heard, ranting and raving about how he'd spent so little time behind bars. I couldn't deny I agreed with him but his intense anger over it didn't help me deal with the situation.

I continued reading.

> They had no hesitation in granting it because he's been such a model prisoner.
>
> As I'm aware of the pitfalls that can befall an inmate when they're released from a correctional facility, I wanted to assist him. He'd expressed an interest in helping us in our work

amongst the marginalised in our local community, especially since it's similar to the neighbourhood he came from.

I think I told you about the program we run here at our church. We offer community services that reach out particularly to families from lower socio-economic backgrounds. We have a number of staff working on this, most on a volunteer basis, although we do have some paid staff. Jeremy is now one of them.

While he hasn't had any official training, he knows better than most of us what these kids are going through, as they have so little hope of advancement it's easier for them to get involved in gangs or crime.

He seems happy and grateful for what we've provided for him and hopefully our work will keep a lot of other kids from treading the path he took.

That's all the news I have for now. Hope to hear from you soon.

Yours truly,

Matt Pearson.

He was out of prison and living a normal life. I supposed he'd just moved on. What had he suffered, anyway? *We* had been the ones who'd suffered.

As stormy as I felt about it, I couldn't get away from what Mel kept telling me. Would a restoration conference really be a good thing? I knew how important it was to move past this, especially if I wanted a career as a social worker. But could I really go through with meeting this guy?

I knew I'd come a long way in the past couple of years. I didn't get as nervous in lonely areas anymore, although I was still more cautious than I had been before my experience. And there was no doubt I wanted it to go away as much as possible, especially so I could do my job.

So that brought me to the only conclusion I could come to. If I wanted to move on completely, it was stupid not to try this restoration conference.

I cringed at the thought of telling Evan. I was talking to him less and less lately, and this topic usually brought out the worst in him. I hadn't seen him for a year, either. He had come up a couple of times but we usually didn't talk about much more than how well we were doing now. It was like we each had to convince the other we were fine. It had become awkward and I hadn't been thrilled to hear he was coming up again. It was hard work dealing with him and this news wouldn't help.

But he deserved to know.

Chapter Seven

Evan had driven up to Brisbane from Sydney and when I saw him I was shocked. He looked thin and exhausted. I tried not to let the alarm show on my face and didn't say anything to him about it, although I was concerned he wasn't well.

He'd driven over, and after a brief hello to my parents, we went out. As he drove along, he turned his tired eyes to me. 'How's study going?'

'Not too bad. It can be challenging, you know.'

I'd told Evan about my placement but had neglected to mention me freaking out in my first counselling session. Fortunately, since then, I'd got better at hiding my reactions to what I heard, although I didn't know if I was any better at dealing with it. Some days it was hard to stay positive.

Evan nodded in approval. 'Think of what you're doing to help these women. I'm glad you've turned all this into something that can help people. It's a sign that good can come from something terrible.'

He didn't sound too convinced of that. I glanced sideways at him. 'How are things for you?'

His reply sounded a little too breezy. 'Oh, just fine.'

'You still working for your brother?'

'No. I decided I needed to branch out. I'm doing accounts for a few different companies now. All small stuff but it's going well. So where do you want to go to eat?'

I tried to ignore his less than subtle change of subject. 'There's a new café I discovered not long ago. Melanie likes it and the food is good.'

'Melanie.'

That was all he said but I could tell from the tone of his voice he hadn't forgiven her for what she'd done. I wisely said no more about her.

We ate without saying much. I kept trying to think of things we could talk about. It didn't seem right to keep going back to what had happened three years before. I settled for talking about the latest movies.

Evan shrugged. 'I don't get to the movies much. Too busy.'

I sighed. What else was I going to say? I kept thinking about the mediation thing but I was sure that would be the biggest conversation killer I could find.

He noticed my distraction, and as soon as we'd finished eating, he suggested we leave. 'Why don't we go down by the river again?'

I smiled. That was a nice idea. It was a little colder than it had been last time but I didn't mind.

We went to pay our bill. Evan pulled out his credit card, but after a moment of trying, the waiter frowned at him. 'I'm sorry, sir, your card has been declined.'

Evan scowled. 'That's ridiculous. There must be something wrong with the machine.'

The waiter tried again but got the same result.

I reached into my bag and pulled out my wallet. 'It's all right. I've got this.'

The waiter looked relieved but Evan's scowl deepened. I ignored him and paid our bill. Then we left.

Although he opened the car door for me Evan said nothing. I could feel hostility emanating from him and felt I needed to say something. 'Sorry. Maybe you need to check your limit.'

'That was completely unnecessary,' he said as he manoeuvred

out into the traffic. 'There was obviously something wrong with the machine.'

'It's all right. You've paid for us every time we've been out. It doesn't matter if I pay for once.'

'Yes it does.'

He didn't say anything else until we arrived at the river and started walking. I was hesitant to take his hand, worried that he would refuse to hold it, but he must have seen my hesitation because he reached out and took it anyway.

'Sorry about before,' he said. 'I just … I don't want you to think I'm not capable.'

I laughed. 'Why would I think that? My card bounces sometimes, believe me.'

He grimaced. 'No. I just … I want to take care of you.'

That made me smile. 'I know. But it doesn't matter if I help out sometimes, does it?'

He sighed and turned towards the railing, looking out over the river. 'You're such a good person, Maddy. You help everyone.'

I wanted to say the same thing about him but I couldn't think of a time when I'd seen him care for anyone but me. However, that was something I could thank him for. 'You help me. You've always helped me. You helped me that night …' I shuddered.

'I helped you? You weren't the one who had to be taken to hospital. No, you were the one who had to deal with them while I was out cold on the floor and—'

He abruptly cut off and a sound like a sob came from his throat. I put my hand on his shoulder. He reached out his arm and pulled me close.

'You don't know how often I think about it,' he said. 'That I left you to deal with them.'

'It wasn't your fault he hit you.'

'Yes it was. I should have given him all the money without hesitation.'

I was shaking my head before he'd finished speaking. 'I honestly think he would have hit you anyway. He wasn't exactly a passive guy, was he?'

He chuckled. 'I guess not.'

I looked at Evan again. Should I bring up the mediation thing? Maybe it would be good for us. These questions tonight made it clear what had happened was still on his mind a lot.

'Evan?' I started out tentatively. 'Do you think that maybe a restoration conference might—'

He whipped his head around to glare at me. 'What are you talking about? Didn't you tell that preacher where to go?'

I contemplated lying but I didn't think he'd believe me. 'No.'

He clenched his fists. 'Don't you see what's going to happen? You listen to that preacher and he's got you right where he wants you.'

'Who, the preacher?'

'No, the crim. He'll be manipulating you next.'

'Come on. A restoration conference is something that can be empowering for the victim—'

'Don't talk to me like you're in class. Or is this just stuff you've picked up from Melanie? She's an interfering busybody who doesn't have the brains to know the right thing to do. Hell, she's too stupid to know a dangerous man when she sees one, that's pretty clear. Look at her history.'

That made me mad. 'Don't talk about Mel that way. You've got no right to judge her for what her husband did to her.'

My words seemed to take the fight out of him. 'I'm sorry. You're right. No one deserves to be treated like that. It wasn't her fault. But don't you see, Maddy? It was the man she was with who was the problem.'

'But not every man is like that.'

'Yes, but you're talking about reconciliation with a guy who's shown he *is* like that! Do you really think it's going to be a success?'

I sighed and looked up at the sky. 'I'd like to think it can. I know that some people don't change, but some do. What if he's one of them?'

'What if he's not?'

'I think I should try anyway.'

He rolled his eyes. 'Maddy, you don't owe him anything.'

'But I owe myself something. If I go and find out he's different, it could be the game changer for me.'

He took my face in his hands. 'I know you think that. You're such a good person; you want to see good in everyone. But it's not always there to find. I don't want to risk him hurting you.'

'It's not like we're going to be alone.'

'Madison, seriously. I don't want anything to do with this guy.'

'What if I do?'

He took a step back. 'I guess that's your decision.'

I groaned. 'Don't be like that.'

'I don't see how else I can be. I don't want you to go and see that guy, and if you're determined to do it …' He shrugged. 'There's nothing more to say.'

No amount of pleading with him would change his mind or his attitude. He took me home shortly after that. He kissed me on the cheek when he left me at the door but seemed in a hurry to get away.

My parents were surprised to see me home at that time. They were sitting around the kitchen table enjoying a cup of coffee and a chat.

'You're home early tonight, Maddy,' Mum said.

The question was implied and I needed to talk to someone. I sat down at the table and put my head in my hands. The tears came more quickly than I would have thought and before long my mum's arms were around me.

'I just don't know!' I yelled in frustration.

'What don't you know?'

'What to do about Evan.'

Dad sighed. 'Things aren't going so well with him, are they?'

'I noticed that he looks quite thin,' Mum said. 'Is he sick?'

'I think his problem is in his head.' I took a deep breath. It was about time I told my parents about the restoration conference. 'Something's upsetting him. Mel's in contact with a prison chaplain in Sydney. He's been working with the guy who held us up.'

Mum looked shocked. 'Why would she contact him?'

'We heard about something called a restoration conference. It's like a mediation. She ... contacted the chaplain for me to find out more about it.'

That thought seemed to unsettle my mum. She gave Dad a guarded look.

'I see,' he said thoughtfully. 'And what do you think?'

'I don't know.'

Mum looked worried. 'Maddy, do you really think that's wise? This man is a criminal.'

I shook my head. 'Yes, and now he's working at this pastor's church, helping him with some neighbourhood kids or something.'

Mum frowned and shook her head. Dad was less easy to read. We both turned to see what he thought. He considered it for a moment. 'But you think this is something you could do?'

I shrugged. 'I'm starting to think I need to.'

'Alan, surely she shouldn't do anything so dangerous!'

Dad waved Mum's protests away. 'Emily, this kind of thing is always done carefully. It's not like Maddy would be left alone with him. They would be closely supervised. And if Maddy thinks this is something she needs to do ...' He looked back at me.

Did I really think I could do this? 'I'll write back to the pastor and see what's involved. I mean, it's still the middle of the semester so I probably can't go down right now.'

Mum nodded, looking relieved. 'That's right. Don't go now, honey. Think about your schooling. That's important too.'

Dad was in agreement. 'Yes, just sound it out with the guy and see what happens. Maybe you can aim at doing something over the summer holidays.'

'I think that's a good idea.' I smiled at them and blinked back the tears. 'Thanks.' I felt better just talking to them about it.

I retreated to my room, and realising I needed to strike while the iron was hot, I logged on to my computer and looked at Mr Pearson's latest email. I gulped as I brought up a new window to reply to him.

Dear Mr Pearson,

I think you know that Melanie Harper has been talking to me about you and the work you do, especially with Mr Stannem. However, the idea of meeting with him is difficult for me to deal with. Part of me thinks I'd be happier never seeing him again but another part of me wonders if I need to.

I definitely need more information. What exactly is involved? I think it will help if I know more about it.

Just so you know, the guy who was in the holdup with me, Evan Mansfield, is very much against this and I don't think that's likely to change. I'm still not sure but I'm curious.

Yours sincerely,

Madison Craig.

I quickly hit 'send' before I could change my mind.

That night I tossed and turned, wondering what it would be like to sit near that resentful face and listen to him try and apologise.

Chapter Eight

I looked up at Aunt Myrtle's federation semi, wondering what had been going on in my head when I'd agreed to do this.

Not long after I'd sent my email I'd received a reply from Mr Pearson. He'd been delighted to hear from me and encouraged me to keep thinking about coming down to see Jeremy Stannem. He gave me details of who I needed to contact in the Department of Corrective Services.

Dad had insisted on contacting them at once. After we'd got some more information from them, Dad, Mum and I had talked about it and I'd eventually decided it was something I needed to do. Dad agreed to come with me and we'd arranged to go over the summer break. So just after Christmas, we'd flown down to Sydney to stay with Aunt Myrtle ... again.

We'd arrived to find her standing on the street with a traffic cone in her hand, saving us a parking spot on the busy road where she lived. She ushered us inside, fussing around as we carried the one suitcase each we'd brought with us. I'd tried to travel light, even though I was staying longer than Dad. He was staying exactly three days. I was planning to stay more than a week, hoping to catch up with Evan, as I hadn't heard anything from him since he'd last been up in Brisbane.

Aunt Myrtle enveloped me in one of her hugs. I could smell incense in her hair.

'Maddy darling, you're so brave.' She held me tightly. 'I know how hard this must be for you. I can't tell you how proud I am that you want to pursue this.'

I gave her a sort of smile and nodded. I didn't want to talk about it. The whole idea scared me to death every time I thought about it.

Mr Pearson had run through the details in one of his emails. He'd asked me if I was happy to have the conference at his church or if I wanted to choose another neutral location, as Jeremy was already comfortable there. But the only place I really knew well in Sydney was Aunt Myrtle's house and I wasn't going to suggest they go there, so I said the church would be fine.

'Don't worry, you'll never be alone with Jeremy,' he'd said. 'When you come down I'll meet with you first so we can go over how the conference will run and you can raise any concerns you have with me then. Feel free to let me know what you would like to get out of the meeting and what you intend to say to Jeremy. I would suggest that you bring someone with you, as well. A supporter.'

I told him my dad was coming and he seemed happy to hear it.

But something worried me. 'Does this mean Jeremy Stannem will have a supporter there too?' I could imagine some other ex-crim glaring at me the whole time I was talking.

Mr Pearson hadn't said anything for a moment and I wondered if we were cut off at first. Then he said, 'He doesn't really have anyone to bring.'

No friends at all? No family? I was still wondering why.

So it looked like it would be okay. I wouldn't have to stay long if I didn't want to. I'd toyed with just telling him he'd ruined my life but that I forgave him and bolting for the door. After all, what more was there to say? Was he going to try and explain why he did it? Claim it wasn't his fault? I knew that's what he'd said in court. He blamed it on Cold Eyes. What would I do if he tried to justify himself?

The following day Matt Pearson came around, more than willing to meet us on 'our turf' since the meeting with Jeremy Stannem was going to be at his church. He was a happy-looking middle-aged guy with a receding hairline and the most open face I'd ever seen. I wondered if he could ever keep a secret. I doubted it.

He shook Dad's hand, then mine. 'Madison, it's a pleasure to meet you at last. I know it hasn't been easy for you to come and we appreciate your bravery. I know Jeremy appreciates it the most. He has felt the guilt of what happened keenly for years now and I know he'd like to tell you himself how badly he feels.'

'Fine.' What else was I supposed to say?

'Now, tomorrow, if the two of you could arrive at about three? Is that okay? We'll hold the meeting in my office. We'll get you two settled, then Jeremy will come in. Jacinta is a social worker at the church and she'll be facilitating the conference. Is there anything you'd like us to cover?'

I shrugged. I couldn't think of anything. The only thing I wanted to know was why he'd done it but I wasn't sure I'd be game enough to ask him, so I kept my mouth shut.

Dad seemed happy with everything so I tried to look like I was too. I was relieved when Matt got up to leave.

Dad looked at me. 'That seemed to go okay.'

'I guess.' It was only the prelude to the terror as far as I was concerned.

Dad drove us to the church. I don't think I could have done it myself. I would have been too tempted to turn around. I squinted at the GPS as it relayed its calm instructions. The air conditioning was blasting but I was still covered with sweat.

I noticed that the streets around us were looking rougher. There were overgrown gardens, front yards filled with what looked like old pieces of cars and some with all sorts of junk everywhere. I knew the suburb the church was in was not in the good end of town. I tried to take deep breaths to calm myself. Whoever had told me that helped was a liar.

Then I noticed that a little flag could be seen in the corner of the GPS. We were nearly there.

I took a deep breath as we turned the corner and saw the church. The neighbourhood around it contained lines of small brick houses, although this theme was broken at one point by a large apartment block that had obviously seen better days. Most of the houses also seemed run down. Many had no fences and those that did, usually had half a fence or one on its way to the ground. I wondered if it was similar inside them.

The church itself was also made of red brick and had a sign out the front that declared it as Westside Community Church. The sign looked as though it had been recently repaired. Unlike other churches I'd seen on the way there, it had no garden. It looked like it had been paved over to make way for a car park that doubled as a basketball court. Some boys were throwing a ball through the hoop as we pulled in at the far end.

As Dad turned off the engine, I looked at the church door. No one was waiting for us. I glanced back at the boys playing basketball. They'd stopped and were watching us.

Dad unbuckled his seat belt. 'Might ask those kids where to go.'

'They'll probably tell you where to go, all right,' I muttered.

'Sorry?'

'Doesn't matter. Let's see if the door's unlocked.'

Before we could make it to the door, I heard a voice, but it wasn't the welcoming one I'd been hoping for.

'Hey you, slut! Old man! What do you think you're doing?'

I looked up to see a kid approaching. To my surprise, I realised she was a girl. She sure looked like a boy. She was stockily built with close cut hair. She flicked the stub of her cigarette away.

I gulped and tried to get a hold of myself. It was difficult, especially as I noticed a group of boys—about four of them—following in her wake.

The girl looked furious as she strode towards us.

Dad didn't seem to notice how aggressive she was. 'Oh, hello. We're here to see the pastor.'

The girl didn't seem to care. She came right up in my face. 'Who said you could come here?'

That got Dad's back up. 'Hey, don't you do that to my daughter.'

I looked around for help. The boys with her hung back, watching with interest.

Facing an adult didn't seem to have any effect on her. 'And who do you think you are, creep? Who said you could just wander in here?' She started poking her finger in his chest.

Before things could escalate any further, the church door swung open and a woman appeared. 'All right, Angel. That's enough. These people are guests.'

Angel? I couldn't think of a name that suited her less.

Angel looked at us through narrowed eyes. 'What are they doing here?'

The other woman held out a hand before she could move any closer. 'You'll have to talk to Jeremy about that later.'

One of the boys spoke up. 'She's that girl, isn't she? The one Jeremy wants to see.' He looked me over like I was a freak.

'Enough. I said you can ask Jeremy about it later. Now get.' With that, the woman gestured that we should go inside and then she shut the door behind us.

I couldn't deny the relief I felt once we were inside the quiet of the church. I looked around. We were in an entry of some sort, not far from two large double doors that were open. From where I was standing I couldn't see what was beyond them, which I guessed was the main part of the church. There wasn't much else in the entryway—just a few chairs, a small table and a cupboard—so I turned my attention to the woman who'd saved us.

It was difficult to guess her age. I thought she was probably in her thirties. She was at least a foot taller than me and was broader than Angel had been. Her black eyes held a friendly look.

'You must be Alan and Madison. I'm Jacinta Mason. Pastor Matt sent me out to meet you.'

She held out her hand and Dad shook it. 'It's nice to meet you.'

'Likewise,' Jacinta said with a smile. 'We're happy you decided to come here today. It means a lot to all of us.'

She began walking and we followed. She led us through the big double doors and I looked around the main part of the church. It was a reasonable size. There was a pulpit thing at the front that was made of wood and looked fairly old. There were some old pews that looked uncomfortable to sit in and also some plastic chairs. All of them were in varying states of disrepair.

Jacinta walked down the aisle in the middle of the church and we followed. She must have noticed me looking around because she began to tell us about it.

'This is a pretty old church and we don't have a lot of money to spend on cosmetic elements.' She gestured to one of the broken pews. 'We prefer to spend what little money we have on other things.'

'Like what?'

'Helping people. I'm sure you noticed that the area we're in is not exactly a rich one. Sometimes we're the difference between a family going hungry and having a good meal.'

As we reached the back of the church, Jacinta pushed a door open. It led to a hallway. There were several more doors and one large window along it.

As we passed the window, I looked through it. It led to what looked like a basketball stadium, but there were chairs banked up on either side. In the middle several tables were set up. Around them were a number of people, mostly senior citizens, packing groceries into boxes.

Jacinta came over to the window where I'd stopped. 'We have arrangements with local supermarkets to take things they have left over. Most of it is a little out of date but still fine. We pack it into boxes and give it to people who need it.'

My eyes widened. There were a lot of boxes. 'How many people do you help?'

Jacinta shrugged. 'As many as possible. It varies from week to week. This has been a good week for donations.'

I looked at the willing volunteers. 'All these people pack it on their own time?'

'Of course. These volunteers know what it's like to need this kind of stuff. Most of them have been in that situation before themselves. They do what they can to help out, knowing that we give back when they need it.'

We continued walking. Jacinta opened a door but didn't go through it. She held it open for us to see.

Inside there were a couple of people going through old clothes and other items.

'We run an op shop as well. Most of that stuff will have a price tag on it, although not much. But we need to have some money coming in to try and keep on top of our other expenses.'

I was impressed. I knew from my placement about how many people benefited from charity work like this.

Jacinta continued down the hall and we followed, with me growing more nervous by the moment. I tried to pull myself together and keep my breathing under control, but it was hard. The idea of being this close to Jeremy Stannem was terrifying.

Jacinta stopped by the door at the end of the hall and rapped her knuckles on it before opening it and gesturing that we should go in before her.

There was only one occupant in the room we entered and it wasn't Jeremy Stannem. The room, which was fitted with cheap-looking wooden panelling, contained a paper-covered desk, a filing cabinet and four chairs. One of the chairs was behind the desk and sitting in it was Matt Pearson.

He jumped up and came around to shake both our hands. 'So wonderful to see you again. I'm glad you found the place okay.'

Dad was at ease. 'You've got a lot of good facilities here and it looks like you use them well.'

Matt shrugged. 'We do our best. I'm not one of those people who wants to facilitate the upkeep of a pretty building. There are more important things to spend money on.'

He gestured to the chairs. 'Please take a seat. Maddy, would you like the chair closest to the door in case you need to take a break?'

Once we were seated, Mr Pearson returned to his seat behind the desk. Jacinta stood against the wall. I tried not to clench my hands in my lap.

Mr Pearson seemed oblivious to my nerves. 'We'll get Jeremy and start in a minute. First, I wanted to check if there's anything you'd like to add since I last saw you?'

I shook my head.

'I think I'll let Maddy and everyone else do all the talking,' my dad said softly. 'I'm just here to be with her and I don't want to interfere in the process.'

'This event touched you too. If you want to tell Jeremy how it affected all your family, feel free to do so.'

Dad looked uncomfortable with that idea. 'We'll see.'

'So when do we start?' I said, trying to keep my voice steady. It was hard work, but I thought I did a creditable job.

Mr Pearson didn't seem to notice anything. 'I want you to be settled before he comes in.'

I didn't see why we shouldn't get it over with, especially while I was still holding it together. I tried to seem casual about it, though, shrugging my shoulders. 'Now is fine.'

'Are you sure? You don't have to yet. We don't want to push you into anything.'

'I don't think it's going to get any easier with waiting.'

I could see him considering that. 'Okay then. Jacinta, can you go and find Jeremy?'

As Jacinta left the room, Mr Pearson turned his eyes back to me. 'Remember, you are free to leave at any point if it becomes too uncomfortable. We're so happy you've come I honestly don't think we'll end the day disappointed and I hope beyond hope this will make you feel better.'

I took a deep breath. 'Sure.' What was the point in disagreeing with him? Besides, I'd come because I wanted some sort of closure. I wanted to be able to move on from this and if that meant talking to this man then that's what I'd do.

The knock sounded on the door again and I gulped. Matt called out 'come in!' and the door opened. Jacinta entered first. Behind her came Jeremy Stannem.

I could feel my heart rate increasing as I looked him over. Jeremy Stannem was only of average height—an inch or two taller than me, no more. I noticed that his dark hair was tied back in the same ponytail but it looked cleaner now than it had been then; not so 'slick'. His dark eyes flickered in my direction but he didn't try to meet my eyes. He looked far more nervous than me. His face seemed to pale further as he looked at Dad, who gazed back calmly.

Jacinta seemed oblivious to any tension in the room. 'Madison and Alan Craig, this is Jeremy Stannem. Why don't we all take a seat?'

Dad was sitting next to me and Jacinta took the chair on the other side of him. Jeremy sat in the chair furthest away. His hands held onto the arms of the chair as though his life depended on it and he wouldn't meet my eyes, not that I stayed looking at him for any length of time.

Jacinta cleared her throat. 'Now Madison, we're here today because of an event a few years ago involving Jeremy, during which time he and another man were responsible for robbing you and a friend at gunpoint in the store where you worked.'

I took in her words carefully. I was glad she hadn't started out by blaming Cold Eyes for what happened, although I was expecting it sooner or later.

'Now, Jeremy has served his allotted time for the crime he committed but still feels considerable remorse for what happened and wanted to tell you in person how sorry he was. Jeremy?'

At the sound of his name, Jeremy raised his nervous eyes from his lap, and for the first time, our eyes met. The moment was so terrifying I looked away immediately. But as I did, I realised something I hadn't expected.

His eyes were different.

Admittedly, his eyes hadn't been the ones I'd remembered most from my ordeal but there had definitely been resentment and restlessness in them before. These eyes were calmer, gentler and the sight of them almost made me gasp out loud. They were so unlike what I was expecting that I started to wonder if this was the same man. I sneaked another peek. No, I was pretty sure it was him. It was a bizarre feeling to have.

I tried to look at him but every time our eyes met I ducked my head. It wasn't long before I noticed he was doing the same.

Eventually, I realised that if this meeting was going to move forward, I had to maintain eye contact with him. I tried to raise my head and keep it there. It was difficult to fight the instinct that said I should look away.

I think Jeremy realised what I was doing and made a conscious effort to do the same. His nerves were still clear, though.

'Miss Craig,' he said. His voice was soft and I tried to remember if this was his normal speaking voice or if it was just the nerves again. I put it down to nerves.

Once he'd said my name he gave a nervous twitch before continuing. 'I know that it probably won't be enough, what I'm going to say.' His hands moved restlessly in his lap. 'I'm sure nothing could really make up for what happened. I'm not going to insult you by trying to tell you it wasn't my fault.'

You were happy to tell that to the judge. I thought it but wasn't game enough to say it.

'I was just as responsible as … my friend for what happened to you. The only thing I really wanted you to know is that I regretted it pretty much from the moment I walked in the door. Again, I know that anything I say won't be enough but I'd like you to know I'm deeply sorry for what happened and if I could go back and stop it, I would.'

Even though his words were uttered softly, once he had finished speaking, I could feel the tears threatening, and although I tried to stop them, before long they were trickling down my cheeks.

I felt Dad's hand on my arm but I couldn't look at him. I couldn't look at anybody. 'Are you all right? Would you like a moment?'

I nodded and Matt rose from his chair. 'Come on, Jeremy, we'll wait outside until Miss Craig is ready.'

I wondered if Jeremy would object but he moved without hesitation. Once the door had shut behind him the tears came more steadily and I began to sob.

Jacinta didn't say anything until I'd recovered enough to apologise.

Dad kept his arm around me. 'Do you want to do this or do you want to go home?'

I knew if I left now, I'd never forgive myself. I wanted to do this and I wanted to do it properly. But it was hard to agree to continue when I knew it was going to be so difficult.

'Do you want Jeremy to come back in or have you had enough?' Jacinta said.

I sighed. I felt an unfamiliar sympathy arise in me for Jeremy. His apology had been unreserved and sincere. Surely I should at least say something to him. 'He can come back in.'

She went to the door and spoke in a murmur. I guessed they hadn't been too far away because both men returned almost immediately and resumed their seats.

'You okay, Madison?' Matt asked.

I nodded, trying to raise my eyes to meet Jeremy's again. His eyes looked stricken and I felt my heart thaw a little in response. He was trying to say sorry. I knew that. I felt I needed to say something to him but I wasn't even sure how to address him. I'd rehearsed with Mel something we felt would be appropriate to use in case I could think of nothing suitable at the time. When she'd mentioned doing that I'd cringed in embarrassment, but now I was glad we had.

'Mr Stannem,' I managed to say. 'Thank you for your apology. I do appreciate it and I'm glad to hear that you acknowledge how terrible it was for us. I'm sure you know how hard it is to forgive this kind of thing and I am trying the best I can because I don't want to carry this weight around in my heart anymore.' A sob strangled my voice, stopping me for a moment. When I could swallow again I continued. 'But I'm sure you can understand the difficulty I have in doing that, both for me and for Evan, my friend. I will try every day, though, because I know it's the only way forward.'

After I'd finished speaking, I dared to look up at him. His gaze was full of compassion and I thought a bit of hope as well. I tried to meet his eyes but I felt more tired than anything and it was hard to even raise my head.

Matt was smiling at me from behind his desk and so was Jacinta. 'That was well spoken, Madison,' she said. She looked at Jeremy.

He glanced at her before turning his eyes back to me. 'Yes it was.' His voice was thick with emotion. 'I'm just relieved you'd even consider forgiving me. You've no idea …' He didn't seem to know what else to say.

We sat in silence for a few minutes. I wondered if that was enough. Could I leave? I darted a look at Matt and then Jacinta.

Matt nodded. 'Was there anything else you wanted to say?'

I shook my head.

'You can say more if you—'

'I think that's it.' I didn't mean to be short but my head was empty of questions and I just wanted to leave.

Matt turned to Jeremy, his eyebrows raised. Jeremy nodded his head but seemed disappointed. As if he knew I wouldn't want to move from my chair with him still in the room, he stood quickly. 'Thank you so much for agreeing to meet with me, Miss Craig. I truly appreciate it.'

With another nod at me, he left the room.

Matt smiled. 'Are you all right, Maddy?'

I shrugged. I didn't know how to answer him. Dad was looking at me intently too. Had that been helpful or not? Should I have said something else? Told him what I thought of him? Yelled at him for a bit? I honestly didn't have the energy.

Jacinta stood. 'Why don't I get you both a cup of tea or coffee?'

My father jumped at the offer. 'Sure. That would be great.' Then he seemed to recollect why we'd come. 'Are you okay with that, Maddy?'

I shrugged. 'Sure.'

I kept quiet as Jacinta led us out of the room. Hopefully by the time the coffee was done Dad wouldn't be too interested in the answers to difficult questions.

Chapter Nine

I had to wonder about Jacinta's sense because she took us straight back into Jeremy's presence. I couldn't shake the feeling that maybe she was too interfering for her own good.

The room we entered had been set up as a café with primitive coffee and tea making facilities, a few cheap biscuits and some cans of soft drink. Some chairs and tables were positioned around, most plastic and mismatched.

What made me uncomfortable, though, were the others in the room, as it was also set up with a couple of pool tables that looked like they'd seen better days, a small gaming station and a few games, books and other things. All of them were being used. There were at least ten kids in the room, varying in age from late teenage to as young as five. All the kids who'd been outside were there, including Angel, who threw me a resentful glare every so often.

I wondered whether Jacinta had intended for us to make our coffees and then go somewhere else, but if so, Dad didn't realise it, because he picked a chair at a nearby table and got settled, looking around the room with interest. He glanced at me, eyebrows raised, when he saw Jeremy on the other side of the room playing a game of pool with one of the older boys, and mouthed *you okay?*

I smiled tersely and took my own seat, careful to keep Jeremy within sight. He didn't seem too thrilled at the sight of me either, if the frown on his face was anything to go by. However, the expression vanished quickly and he went on with what he was doing.

Jacinta didn't seem to notice any of this and sipped her coffee casually. 'Coffee is the best invention I think the human race ever had,' she said. 'Nothing can soothe a worry away quite like a cup of coffee.'

'You're right there,' my father replied. I didn't answer, intent on finishing my drink. Once I'd done that, we were leaving.

Jacinta turned to me. 'So Maddy, what do you do? Work or study?'

'I'm studying social work.'

Her eyes lit up. 'Really? What are you planning to do once you've graduated?'

I shrugged, wondering if she'd be as discouraging as Melanie. 'I was hoping to do something with victims of crime.'

She nodded. 'That's understandable, given what you've been through. What year are you?'

'About to start my fourth.'

'You've done placement, then?'

I told her a little about my time at the domestic violence unit. To my surprise, I started to relax. No matter what I told her, she didn't seem shocked or disapproving, even when I mentioned running out of the room in counselling. Instead, she laughed. 'I can well imagine that. Some of that stuff is hard-core.'

She turned to my father. 'Do you have any other children?'

'None.' I could hear a trace of sadness in his voice. 'My wife had difficulties in that area.'

She sighed. 'It's always the good parents who seem to have the most trouble. I don't know why that is. It's the kind of thing that makes it hard for me to believe in what this church teaches.'

My dad puffed up at her praise but she didn't seem to notice. She nodded to a kid sitting in a corner of the room playing with the X-Box. 'See that boy? That's Sean. He lives with his aunt a few streets away. He was sent there because both his parents were struggling with severe addiction and his mother was dealing from home. All his other siblings—all four of them—went to other family members. None of them are local.

Unfortunately, his aunt isn't what you'd call a great influence. She plies him with alcohol all the time. We've tried to work with her and have made several reports to child protective services but they don't have the resources to investigate something that isn't a serious and immediate risk.'

I looked at the boy. His clothes were worn out but he seemed to be engaging with the others in a normal manner. 'He doesn't look too bad.'

'He's been better since he's started coming here. It gives him something to do. It's hard in the evening, though, when he has to go home. Jeremy tries to keep him here as late as possible, in the hope that his aunt will have passed out by the time he gets home. It's better that way.'

The shock of Jeremy's sudden appearance in the conversation was pushed out of my mind at the thought of a child being kept away from home until the adult figure in his life was unconscious. I had become all too aware of things like that in the past year or so, but it was still difficult to hear about kids who were forced to live like that. 'How old is he?'

'Twelve.'

Again, it wasn't unheard of but it was still hard to take.

'And that's Bodin.' She pointed to the kid playing pool with Jeremy. 'He's a good kid. Determined to do the right thing. Wants to go to school and get into uni so he can be a doctor. Don't know if he's got the brains for it, unfortunately, or the level of commitment something like that would take. I don't like to be discouraging, though. He's had it rough. His mum cleared out when he was five and his dad doesn't do much more than get drunk and bring a continuing parade of women home to play house.'

'His mum left and didn't take him with her?' my father asked.

'We're not sure exactly. It's difficult to tell what happened to her. We've looked for her, for Bodin's sake, but haven't been able to find her.'

I looked at the only girl in the room, who was still scowling at me on a regular basis. 'What about Angel?'

Jacinta grinned. 'She's a challenge. She's taken up smoking recently to try and help overcome her drug habit. She's been in and out of rehab for a while. It seems to be working but sometimes she's difficult to help because she's so aggressive. She pushes away any opportunity to engage with her in more than a rudimentary way. You probably noticed she doesn't like other girls being here. That's why there aren't any. We do have others who come now and then, but only when Angel's not here.'

As I put down my coffee on the table, I spilled a little and the now-cool liquid sloshed onto the table. 'Damn.' I looked around for a washcloth or something to clean it up with.

Before I could get up, I sensed a presence at my elbow. It was the youngest person in the room—a little boy. He had the most beautiful, innocent big blue eyes. He held up a cloth to me with a smile.

'Let me help,' he said, lifting my cup by the handle carefully and cleaning under it. 'See? Good as new.' He grinned at me.

I was overwhelmed at this sweetheart coming to my aid. 'Thank you so much.'

To my astonishment, he leant in and hugged me. He held on tightly, almost as if he were afraid to let go. Then he smiled and went back to a corner where he had been reading some books.

I looked back at Jacinta and she smiled. 'I see you've been charmed by Rory.'

I raised my eyebrows. 'Why? Was all that innocence an act?' I wondered if I needed to check my bag to see if my wallet was still there.

She laughed. 'No, not at all. But he's a little charmer. Fortunately, with him it's genuine.'

'What's his story?'

'A sad one.' Jacinta looked down and ran her fingers down the side of her coffee cup. I guessed it must be terrible if it affected her. She seemed to take things in her stride. 'His parents were killed in a car crash when he was two. Since then, he's been to several different members of his family. Went to Grandma first, then she died of cancer. Then he went to an uncle who hit him. Now he lives with a second cousin. She's not a bad woman but she prefers it when he's not around. There are occasions when she treats him like he's precious but it doesn't last long. She acts like he's a doll she can put on the shelf and only get out when she wants him. I guess I can understand—their relationship isn't close and she's only twenty-two—but I feel sad for him.

'He's better since he's started coming here. He used to cry all the time but now he seems happier, and as you can see, he'll do just about anything for anyone.'

How sad his life had been! It made my own hardship seem like nothing in comparison. My eyes darted to Jeremy, where he was still playing pool. Did he have a similar story?

I put that from my mind, and as Jacinta was distracted by Angel, who had just thrown her coffee into the face of the boy next to her and had started screaming at him, I gave my dad a glance. He raised his eyebrows but said nothing as I got up and went over to where Rory was reading. I knelt down beside him. 'Hello again.'

He smiled up at me. 'Hello.'

I looked at the book. It was a storybook with pictures but it looked a little beyond his reading level. Nevertheless, he was squinting at the pages.

'Can you read?' I asked.

He shook his head. 'I'm learning at school, though.'

'How old are you?'

'Six.'

A lot of terrible things had been packed into those six years. 'Would you like me to read to you?'

His eyes lit up. 'Yes, please!'

I sat on a beanbag on the floor and Rory took no time in settling on my lap. There I sat for the next hour or so, going through book after book with him. I forgot about why I was there and simply enjoyed seeing the delight on his face as he looked at the pictures and tried to follow along with the story.

Jacinta eventually came over to us. My dad had come over too, watching me with a grin on his face.

'Rory, I think it might be time to have some dinner,' Jacinta said. 'How about we go and get some?'

He got up immediately and took her hand. Looking around, I noticed that the room was emptying quickly. 'You give them dinner?'

'Not every night. We try and do it a couple of times a week.'

'Where?' Wouldn't it have made more sense to serve it in the café?

'Come and I'll show you.'

She led me to the wall that cut the auditorium in two and went through a door in it. The room where the volunteers had been packing groceries before had changed. The two rows of tables were still set up but were no longer covered with boxes and tins of food. Instead, there were plates containing sandwiches, sausage rolls, party pies, vegetable sticks and fruit.

Everyone grabbed a plate from the end of one of the tables and filed past, loading their plates with food, before taking it back to the café area.

Jacinta handed my father and me two plates. 'Here, have some.'

'Oh, we can't do that,' Dad said. 'This food is for the needy. We hardly qualify on that score.'

I heard a scornful sound and noticed Angel looking our way. I turned back to Jacinta.

'Maybe you should accept our hospitality for today,' she said.

Dad turned and looked at Angel too, before turning back to me. 'What do you think, Maddy?'

I shrugged my consent as Rory came up beside me and began

advising me on what was best to eat. When we returned to the café, he set his plate at our table and talked non-stop about all the fun he had at the church. I was surprised at how much they did. I was also surprised that my nerves had gone and I wasn't even looking at Jeremy anymore, where he sat with the older boys on the other side of the room.

I was noticing Angel more and more, though. She was practically snarling at me from where she sat. I could tell Jacinta saw it too. She ignored it so I decided I would too.

Eventually, my presence must have been too much for her.

'How long is she staying here?' she said loudly, not talking to anyone I could see. 'Why's she here anyway? And who's the old man, her sugar daddy?'

I bristled at that but my father just snorted good-naturedly.

'Maddy and her father came to see Jeremy,' Jacinta replied.

'Well, there he is.' She stabbed her finger at Jeremy, who was watching her silently. 'She's seen him now. I think it's time for her to leave.'

No one said anything but Jeremy's face was getting darker by the moment.

'Come on, slut, get out of here now.' She picked up the knife she'd been using to eat. 'While you still can.'

She got up from her place and strode towards me. Dad got up to meet her but she never made it that far. Jeremy had risen from his seat, vaulted over the table and grabbed her by the arm with a pincer-like grip.

With one hand on her shoulder and the other on the arm holding the knife, he shook her arm until she dropped it. She began to curse at him, yelling words I'd never even heard before but I was pretty sure they weren't compliments. He ignored all her protests and led her towards the door, dragging her along and shutting it behind them.

My heart was thumping and took a while to settle down after that. Jeremy returned about half an hour later without Angel. I wondered what had happened to her.

The odd thing was, I hadn't been worried about her safety so much as Jeremy's. She'd seemed the more dangerous of the two.

What did that mean? Did it mean anything at all?

It was getting late and I was about to tell Dad it was time to go home when one of the boys approached. At first I was nervous; what if his reaction was the same as Angel's? But Jacinta didn't seem worried so I looked up at him. I couldn't recall seeing him before.

'This is Brett,' Jacinta said when he was standing before us.

To my surprise, Brett held out his hand for me to shake. He was fairly tall but looked young, although I couldn't tell exactly how young. He had sandy-coloured hair and quizzical hazel eyes. Judging by his first question, he was also direct. 'You're that girl who Jeremy held up, aren't you?'

I gulped, not sure where this was going. 'Yes, I am.'

He cocked his head. 'Why are you here?'

'Uh.' I looked at Jacinta. 'Well, that's hard to explain.'

He pulled up a chair and sat backwards on it. 'So explain it to me.'

His manner didn't seem aggressive but it was intense and it frightened me a little.

Jacinta stepped in. 'Brett, given how much detail you'll want, I don't think we should go there now.' She looked at her watch. 'It's getting late so it's probably time you went anyway.'

I nodded. She didn't sound like she was dismissing us, more like helping us out of a tough situation. Maybe Brett wouldn't be as friendly once he'd heard what I had to say.

When I looked at him for his reaction I thought I might be right. There was a scowl on his face. 'What? Is she scared?' He gave me a withering look. 'Does she really think Jeremy is going to do anything to her? I mean—*Jeremy?*' He made it sound like it was impossible to imagine. He turned to Jacinta. 'This is just some setup you and Preacher have put together, isn't it? Give me a break.'

His voice wasn't loud but his eyes were fierce and I shrank back. Jacinta did not. 'It's no trick, Brett. It's the truth.'

Brett turned his antagonistic glare back to me. 'Then she can tell me about it.'

I looked at Jacinta. 'I'm okay with—'

She held up her hand. 'No. If you get started on this now, you'll be here half the night.'

I looked at Brett. I didn't think he was a bad kid in spite of the tough look on his face. And it irked me that he thought I was lying. 'Well, maybe I could come back some other day. When are you free, Brett?'

Dad gave me a sharp look, even though I'd kept my question light and unconcerned. Brett narrowed his eyes at me, as if measuring whether I really meant what I said. I stared him down.

After a minute, he looked unconcerned. 'Sure. I'll be here tomorrow all afternoon.'

I frowned. I'd hoped to try and find Evan then, and Dad was going back to Brisbane in the afternoon. But I felt Brett was throwing down a challenge. If I wanted to earn his respect I'd have to take it up. 'I'm free tomorrow afternoon. How about I come at two?'

'Whatever.' Brett walked away without another word.

When he'd gone, I turned to Dad. 'You okay with that?'

He seemed surprised but not upset by what I'd done. 'It's your decision, darling. You know I'll be at the airport by then so I won't be able to come with you. Are you happy to come here on your own?'

I tried to keep my voice confident. 'Yes, I think so.'

Jacinta frowned. 'You don't have to do this, you know. Brett has some issues where Jeremy is concerned. With all of us, actually. He's not likely to believe anything you say.'

I sighed. 'It doesn't matter. I may as well tell him. If he chooses not to believe, that's his problem.'

She grinned. 'Okay. I'll be here tomorrow afternoon. I'll see you then.'

'Will Jeremy be here?' I wasn't sure if I wanted to see him again, but then, maybe he could help convince Brett. And maybe I'd think of a few of the things I was sure I'd wanted to tell him. I was bound to remember them the moment I walked out the door.

She looked across the room at him. He was watching us but looked away when we turned towards him. 'Yes, he should be here.'

I nodded. 'Maybe he'll believe both of us.'

***

On the way home Dad asked a couple of times if I was okay about going back the next day. I must have sounded convincing, because he seemed satisfied by the time we reached Aunt Myrtle's, even though my stomach churned at the thought of what I'd agreed to do. Although Jeremy hadn't been threatening in any way, it was still unnerving to see him, even if it was hard to see much resemblance between him and the guy in my memories.

When we pulled up outside Aunt Myrtle's, I saw the curtain flutter. My father grimaced. 'We should have let her know we were going to be late. She's probably been worried sick.'

She was sitting in her favourite chair when we walked in. 'You're later than I expected. Are you hungry? I saved you some dinner.'

'Sorry, Myrtle,' Dad said. 'We should have called. We've already eaten.'

She didn't seem too concerned about the food, turning to her more pressing question. 'How did it go?'

At her question, Dad turned to me too, but I was still trying to work out what the answer was. It had seemed to go okay. Jeremy seemed genuinely apologetic and I'd felt less afraid of him than I would have expected. I was still in two minds about my return visit, though. 'It went okay. In fact, I'm going back tomorrow.'

'Why?'

I gave a little laugh. 'Because one of the kids there didn't seem to buy my story.'

'What kids?'

We gave her a quick rundown on the things the church did in

the neighbourhood. 'There was one boy who challenged me on why I was there. He seems to think it never happened at all.'

'Well, you can take these then.' Aunt Myrtle stood up and went into the hall, coming back with a folder. Inside, I was surprised to find a few newspaper clippings relating to the armed robbery and what had happened. I felt nauseated at the sight of a picture of Cold Eyes but I was drawn to the picture next to him—the picture of Jeremy.

I could immediately see why there was so little resemblance between the man I'd seen today and the one in this photo. While he looked more scruffy and unkempt, it was the look in his eyes that made all the difference. My memory hadn't been playing tricks on me. This face was definitely more resentful than the guy I'd met today.

What had changed him? I didn't know but suddenly I was determined to find out.

Chapter Ten

When I hopped out of the car in the church car park, Aunt Myrtle's scrapbook was tucked under my arm. Maybe I was being defensive but I didn't like that Brett had decided what I'd been through was all made up. Why would anyone do something like that?

I was using Aunt Myrtle's car this time. It wasn't flash, so hopefully no one in this neighbourhood would try to steal it.

Just like the day before, Angel and a couple of the guys were there. Being without Dad made it even more frightening than it had been then. I braced myself for Angel's taunts but this time she kept her distance, watching me with a sour look on her face. I would have ignored them if I hadn't noticed that Brett was there.

He came up to me as I reached the door, the others following in his wake. When he reached me, he looked me up and down, an arrogant expression on his face. He glanced at the scrapbook. 'What's that? Baby pictures?'

I met his eye. 'Nope. Evidence.'

I didn't engage him further and knocked on the door. Jacinta must have been waiting just inside because she opened it almost immediately. However, before she could say anything, Angel spoke up. 'The door's not locked, you know. You can just walk in.' She rolled her eyes. 'What, do you think this is a bank or something?'

'That's enough, Angel,' Jacinta said. 'Come in, Maddy. You're very welcome.'

I was nervous as I entered, as I assumed that Jeremy wouldn't be too far away and I was worried about seeing him again. To my surprise, I couldn't see him anywhere. While I didn't expect him in the main part of the building, where they did the actual church stuff, I expected him to be in the split auditorium, but he wasn't. There were a few other kids though, Rory among them. His eyes lit up as soon as he saw me and he came over to give me a hug. I hugged him back. It was nice to get a warm welcome from one of the kids.

Once his hug was over he went and got a storybook and brought it back for me to read, but Jacinta shook her head. 'Sorry, Rory. Maddy can't read just now. She's here to talk to Brett and some of the others today.'

A chair had been set up with a semicircle of other chairs around it. Jacinta waved me towards the single chair, which made me nervous, especially as all the kids started taking seats in the other chairs. I hadn't realised this was going to be so formal. I'd thought I'd just tell Brett what had happened, show him the book and leave it at that. I didn't expect there would be others who would listen to what I had to say. And while some of them had bored looks on their faces, I thought I could detect glimmers of interest everywhere.

I sat down hesitantly and looked around at them. To my relief, Jacinta took over.

'Okay,' she said. 'Some of you heard from Jeremy why Maddy came to see him yesterday. You guys already know Jeremy's done time. I know some of you choose not to believe it. After all, he's way too nice for an ex-con, isn't he? And then Maddy shows up and Jeremy tells you that she's the one he hurt with his crime. You don't believe that either. Because this forgiveness thing doesn't actually ever happen, does it?

'Well, apparently it does, because Maddy was willing to do it. She's going to tell you her story. I want you to listen to it without interrupting. If you want to ask questions you can wait until she's done. If you think it's crap and you want to walk out, you can do that too. We don't want you here if you don't want to listen. But if you're staying, you stay quiet until Maddy says so. Got it?'

There were snorts and grumbles and plenty of eye rolling.

'Like I said, you're free to go now if you don't want to hear this. If you're staying, I expect you to respect Maddy. You all know that word. You want it for yourselves. Show you deserve it by offering it to someone else.'

No one left, although they didn't look happy about staying, either. Jacinta turned to me and indicated that I should start.

I gulped. 'Okay. I don't know what … Jeremy—' it was hard to say his name out loud— 'has told you, but about four years ago I was working in a bookstore-slash-cafe here in Sydney with another guy. It was at the end of a really busy day. We'd done well, what with all the customers who'd come through, but it had quietened down in the lead-up to closing time, and we were winding down when two men came in.'

My hands started to shake. It usually happened when I got to this part of the story. I hoped my voice wouldn't shake too much. This was hard enough as it was. 'I thought they were customers at first, but one of them pointed a gun at me and told me to hand over the money in the till. I was about to do that when Evan, the guy I was working with, came back. He'd just gone to get something from out the back.

'They threatened him as well, and he got the money out for them.' I skipped the bit where Jeremy had held the gun to my temple. I wasn't sure I could handle saying that bit. 'Anyway, the other guy, not Jeremy, still bashed my friend with the gun and he fell down, unconscious. Then …' I hesitated. Could I tell them about Cold Eyes dragging me towards the door? I'd never told anyone that, not even the police. I hadn't even been able to remember it when they'd interviewed me. It had only come back to me afterwards.

I looked around to see if Jeremy was watching. I couldn't see him anywhere. I took a deep breath and kept going.

'So they took the money but there were some people walking

along the street when they went to leave, and they got the licence plate of their car. That meant the police were able to follow them. From what I heard, and Jeremy can probably tell you better than me what happened then, they crashed the car. The cops caught Jeremy, but the other guy decided to put up a fight, and they shot him.'

There was silence as I ended my story. It stretched on for a few minutes until I wondered if anyone was going to say anything. Their expressions varied from thoughtful to disbelieving.

Eventually, Brett spoke. 'So why don't you hate Jeremy?'

Angel nodded. 'Yeah, with what he did to you, you shouldn't be here for any other reason than to kill him.'

Her blunt assessment shocked me into being more honest than I intended. 'What good would killing him do? How does that fix what I have to live with day after day?'

Brett leant forward, his face intense. 'What *do* you have to live with?'

That was not an easy thing to talk about. 'Before this happened to me I was so … carefree. I didn't think bad stuff would happen. I was optimistic. I was probably naïve as well.

'I guess it was inevitable I would find out sooner or later that life wasn't a bed of roses. But not like *that*. After it first happened I was afraid to walk down the street alone. Going to work was a nightmare, especially if it was getting dark. And at first if I saw people who look like them, it made me feel sick to my stomach.

'Then there's the disconnect. Knowing that no one else around you understands what it is to feel like that. I know you know what it's like to suffer. You probably think what I went through isn't much. I could understand that. But at least you can talk to people here and they know what it feels like to be there. No one I knew had any idea what this was like. Within a few weeks, they'd forgotten it had even happened. But I never did. I lived with it day after day after day.'

'Then why did you come here to forgive Jeremy?' Brett asked. 'If he's done that to you, then why not just hate him?'

I shook my head. 'I realised I don't want to live with that kind of hate in me. I don't think it would do me any good. I learnt that when we discussed dealing with trauma at uni but I think I knew it myself. I didn't like the way I felt when I hated him.'

'What about the other guy?' Angel said. 'The guy in the bookstore with you?'

I sighed. 'He wants nothing to do with Jeremy. His reaction is pretty much what you're talking about.'

Angel cocked her head. 'How's he going with that?'

'I don't know. I haven't seen him in a while.' I was hoping to change that in the next couple of days, if I could find out where Evan was living.

Brett shot to his feet, his chair shooting back so it almost hit the wall a few metres away. Then he stalked out of the room.

I watched him go and wondered what I'd said wrong. I glanced at Jacinta but she didn't seem too concerned.

There were no more questions. Some of the kids seemed to be pondering what I was saying. I pulled out the scrapbook and showed them the clippings Aunt Myrtle had kept. They definitely recognised Jeremy and muttered between themselves as they looked at his picture.

I looked down and Rory was back by my side. He grinned. 'Is it story time now?'

***

I must have read Rory thirteen books before I could get away. I hadn't intended to stay that long. I'd been hoping to find someone who could give me Evan's contact details. Aunt Myrtle thought that Michael, who used to own the bookstore, might know. He'd sold it a couple of years before but my aunt had kept in touch with him. She'd been going to check if he knew where Evan was.

Jacinta fell in step with me as I headed out. 'Thanks so much for coming today.'

I shrugged. 'I don't know if it did any good.'

'You might be surprised.'

She walked me to the car. When we arrived in the car park, I noticed Brett was there, playing one-on-one basketball with Jeremy. It was the first time I'd seen him that day.

By the sweat pouring from their faces and their looks of exhaustion, I thought that they'd been playing for a while. I watched Brett, wondering what had motivated his interest in my story, not to mention his sudden departure.

To my surprise, both of them approached as I put my things in my car. Jeremy hung back further, although Brett didn't seem keen to come too close without him. In spite of Jacinta's presence, he kept looking back to see where Jeremy was. I tensed, even though his face didn't look threatening in any way.

'Um, I was wondering if I could say something,' Brett mumbled as he came up to my car. He wouldn't look me in the eye, instead he looked down as he kicked one of my tyres with his foot.

I waited for Brett to speak.

It came out suddenly. 'I think you're pretty brave.' He looked me in the eye as he said it. 'It takes a lot of guts to do something like that. I know. I …'

He seemed about to continue, then dropped his head and walked away. I looked to Jacinta first, then Jeremy for an explanation.

He began after a moment of silence. 'Please excuse him. He's going through some hard stuff at the moment. You coming here has made him face some things he doesn't want to face.'

'Oh.' That was all I could think to say.

Jeremy nodded. 'I won't go into the details, but let's just say he'd like someone's forgiveness but he needs to offer it to someone else as well. You—'

I heard a curse from behind us as Brett returned. 'I don't need to offer anyone anything.'

Jeremy gave him a sceptical look.

Brett's face turned haughty. 'It's the truth and you know it.'

He walked up to Jeremy and shoved him, but he just stood there while Brett snarled in his face.

'Brett …' Jacinta's voice was cautionary but didn't seem to have any effect.

It was then I noticed the discarded basketball and wondered if I could distract him. Uni had taught me that distraction could be useful in diffusing a tense situation. I walked over and picked up the ball.

As soon as my hands were on it Brett snorted. 'A girl who can play basketball?'

What was he, a Neanderthal? 'They do have basketball teams full of girls, you know. And in this country too.' I wasn't sure I should speak like that to Brett, considering there were issues he was obviously not dealing with that had been stirred up by my presence, but I was tired of walking on eggshells.

He rolled his eyes. 'You've played in one, I guess?'

'Nope. I played netball in school, though.'

He smirked. 'Netball. Oh, that's so cool!'

I narrowed my eyes but didn't bother to reply. Instead, I turned and stalked towards the basketball hoop. When I was three metres away I took aim, praying my shot was still good, and let the ball fly. It glided smoothly through the hoop and bounced onto the tarmac.

I turned back to the others to see them gaping at me. I'm sure I looked smug. 'Netball does teach you how to shoot, you know.'

Jacinta laughed and clapped her hands.

I bounced the ball back to Brett. He glanced at Jeremy. 'What do you reckon? Do we take her on?'

Jeremy didn't seem too keen on the idea. He glanced at Jacinta.

'Maybe you two should fight it out between yourselves,' she said.

'Sure thing, lady.'

'Maddy,' I said.

It was a close match. I was able to shoot from a distance but Brett had a considerable height advantage so could get more baskets that way, but he had to be close enough. He was hopeless at shooting from any distance.

In the end he beat me, but only just. Even as he walked away with the light of victory on his face I could see a respect there as well.

'Didn't know girls could shoot hoops,' he said.

'I guess Angel doesn't play basketball.'

I wasn't really talking to anyone when I said that and I was a little surprised when Jeremy answered in a low voice. 'She's not really the sporty type.'

He and Jacinta had been leaning against the wall, watching our entire match. As the game ended, Jacinta came up and high-fived me. 'Hopefully that's one lesson he will remember.'

I was a little nervous about Jeremy's presence but tried not to show it. He was behaving like a normal human being. I knew I needed to do that too. I smiled at both of them. 'Yeah, he needs to learn that not all girls are deficient when it comes to sport.'

To my surprise, Jeremy chuckled. 'I think he might have just done that.'

Then his face turned serious. He glanced at Jacinta before turning back to me. 'You know, they all appreciated you coming back here today to talk to them. They were really interested to hear your story. I know it can't have been easy for you to come.'

I tried to keep my voice casual. 'I'm glad I could be of help but I'm not sure they cared. Some of them, anyway.'

'Maybe, maybe not,' Jacinta said. 'Most of these kids have been involved in crime of some form or other. If they haven't broken the law, then someone else in their family has. And sometimes they've been the victims.'

Jeremy gestured to where Brett had disappeared. 'He's had his own brushes with the law. There was …' He stopped before he could tell me the details. 'Anyway, I know he'd like forgiveness from someone, even though he pretends he doesn't.'

'Did he hurt them?'

'He did and he's served time in a juvenile justice centre for it.'

'Juvenile justice centre.' It sounded like a slap on the wrist to me.

He must have picked up on my tone. 'They're not fun places, you know.'

Jeremy's reply felt like a rebuke even though it was uttered calmly. And I couldn't deny I deserved it. 'Sorry. That was rude.'

The moment the apology was out of my mouth he was backpedalling. 'No, I'm sorry. I shouldn't be … I don't mean to be defensive.' He looked back and forth from me to Jacinta. 'These kids just mean a lot to me. This whole place means a lot to me.'

His eyes were so earnest. Could he really be one of those people who were rehabilitated?

'I'd like to thank you again for coming here yesterday,' he continued. 'I appreciate that you were willing to do that.'

I wasn't sure we'd achieved a great deal in our session but he seemed to have benefited from it. Perhaps the mere fact I was standing there talking to him meant I had too. 'I'm glad I could help.'

Things were getting awkward so I felt it was time to leave. 'I should be getting home.'

'Thanks again for coming today,' Jacinta said.

'Well, don't expect me tomorrow. I've got another friend to visit.' I hoped I did, anyway.

Jeremy cocked his head. 'The other guy from the robbery?'

'Yes.'

He nodded and shoved his hands in his pockets. 'Tell him I'm sorry too. I know he probably won't accept it but I want to be sure he knows it's offered.'

I sighed. 'He knows, but I'll tell him anyway. See you later, Jacinta. And thank you, Jeremy.'

It was only as I started the engine that I realised I'd used his first name in his presence for the first time. It was a weird feeling but it didn't upset me. I didn't know what to make of that.

Chapter Eleven

Aunt Myrtle was, again, waiting when I got home.

'Glad you're not as late as last time,' she said, as she laid my dinner before me at the table.

'So am I.' Although I couldn't deny I'd enjoyed myself. Or was that really the right word for it? Satisfied was a better way to put it. On the way home I'd reflected on my game with Brett and the fact that I'd been able to talk sensibly to Jeremy. That had to be a step in the right direction.

I told Aunt Myrtle about the day's activities and she seemed to share my opinion. 'I'm glad you've found a way to talk to that young man. It must be a weight off his mind.'

I shrugged. 'I guess it must be.'

Aunt Myrtle changed the subject. 'Now, I've been doing a little research myself today. I got onto Michael and he gave me Evan's brother's contact details.'

I pricked up my ears. 'Evan used to work for him.' I knew that, but Evan had never even told me his name so I didn't know how to contact him.

Aunt Myrtle looked serious. 'From what Michael said, I'm not sure his brother has even been in contact with him. Apparently he's in quite a bad way.'

'Do you mean he's sick?' If that was the case, I was visiting him immediately. I got up from the table.

She held out her hand. 'Now, don't be hasty. He's not sick, no. Not physically, anyway. He's just … well, apparently he's letting himself go a bit.'

'In what way?'

'Not sure, dear. That's just what I was told.'

There was only one thing I could think of that was behind it, and it wasn't like I hadn't seen signs of it myself. I put out my hand for the paper she held out to me, determination in my eyes.

She must have read my face. 'You're not going there now, and that's final. Look at the neighbourhood he's in.'

I checked the paper. To my surprise, he lived not too far from Westside church. That was a shock. I was sure he'd move if he knew he was that close to Jeremy.

Unless … A shiver of fear shot up my spine. What if Evan knew where Jeremy was? Would he do something to hurt him? Surely not. And if he did know and intended to do anything, wouldn't he have already done it? Yes, I was sure of that. Well, not completely sure, but I tried to convince myself. Evan wouldn't hurt Jeremy. He must realise it would do no good!

Aunt Myrtle sighed with relief as my face calmed. 'That's right. No need to race over there now. The morning will come soon enough.'

***

The next morning I headed around there bright and early. I was horrified when I saw where he was living. It was an apartment complex but the different apartments looked so run down I couldn't believe he'd even considered them as a place to live. And the neighbourhood was scarier than Westside's. Although there was a visitors' car park right near the complex, there was also a bunch of kids nearby and I worried about the safety of Aunt Myrtle's car. I smiled at them as I parked and tried not to shake as I turned my back on them, but I was listening behind me for any sound they made. I had a quick look for witnesses. There was an old man raking leaves in the complex's front yard. He came up to me as I approached.

'Looking for someone, missy?' he asked.

'Yes, I'm looking for Evan Mansfield. I believe he lives here in apartment twenty-five.'

The old man narrowed his eyes. 'Yes, I think I know the fellow. Not sure he's home. Just take the lift up to the fifth floor and you should find him.'

I thanked the man and couldn't stop myself glancing at my car before I went inside.

The old man noticed. 'Don't worry, love. I'll watch your car for you.'

I smiled. 'Thank you.'

The ride in the lift was terrifying. The doors groaned like they were in pain as they closed and the trip up five floors took forever and was accompanied by the sound of grinding machinery. I was sure I would plummet to the ground any second. I considered taking the stairs on the way down.

When I stepped out of the lift I didn't feel much better. The floor I was on was grimy and unkempt. Fortunately, Evan's apartment wasn't far down the hall.

No one answered my knock. I stayed in front of the door for a while, hoping that he was just asleep or showering or something, but nothing happened. I considered leaving a note and slipping it under the door but I didn't have a paper or pen.

As risky as it was, I took the lift down again. The stairwell looked even more frightening and was filled with rubbish.

As I walked out I noticed with relief that my car was in one piece. The man was still raking. 'Wasn't there, love?'

I shook my head.

'He's usually out on Thursdays. I think he has work or something. Try again tomorrow. He should be home then.'

I smiled my thanks and hurried back to the car. Now what was I going to do? I'd planned to spend the day with Evan, although I could sense some relief that that wasn't going to happen now, especially if it meant being in this neighbourhood. I didn't want to go and spend the day with Aunt Myrtle and I hadn't sought out anyone else who had worked in the bookstore. I'd always been afraid of seeing them again in case they noticed some kind of change in me or pitied me. I didn't want pity.

My thoughts turned to the little church at Westside. It was only five minutes away. Could I pop around there? Did I want to? I thought of Brett. Would he think me brave or annoying if I showed up today? What would Jeremy think? Maybe it would relieve his guilt a bit more. I realised I wanted to do that. I thought of Rory waiting with his books.

Then another thought occurred to me. Rory deserved some nice new books. It was a pity Your Corner Bookstore was so far away. Was there another bookstore somewhere nearby?

Once I was in the safety of my car I pulled out my phone and searched the internet. There was one about fifteen minutes away. It was a bit out of the way but I felt it would be worth it to see the smile of delight on Rory's face.

About forty-five minutes later I arrived at the church with a bag of books in each arm. Jeremy was in the car park playing basketball with Brett, Bodin and another boy I didn't know. They looked up in surprise as they realised who it was.

'Hey, it's the hoop-shooting girl!' Bodin said. He came over and peered in the bags I was carrying. 'Watcha got?'

I appreciated that he was so upbeat. He'd seemed disinterested in what I'd said the day before but apparently didn't hold it against me. 'It's not for you,' I chided, trying to keep my voice light.

Brett hung back a bit but Jeremy came forward without too much hesitation. 'What is it?'

'I thought that Rory deserved some new books.' I let him see inside the bags.

He looked up at me, shocked. 'These are brand new.'

I shrugged. 'May as well spend my money on a good cause. I hope they're okay. It's been a while since I've worked in a bookstore.' My voice faltered a little as I said that. In fact, it had been difficult for me to walk through the front door, even though it looked nothing like Your Corner Bookstore. I hadn't been to any bookstore since what had happened to me.

Jeremy must have heard the tremor in my voice as the look he gave me was filled with sympathy and guilt. I tried to steady my voice. I wasn't there to make him feel bad. 'Well, I'd better get these inside. They're pretty heavy.'

He immediately reached for the bags and took them from me. 'Here, let me help.'

'You don't have to do that,' I protested.

'It's all right. Wow, they are heavy.'

I wasn't sure if he was just saying that to make conversation. Whatever the reason, I appreciated his effort. 'Books can be, you know.'

'I'd guess you'd know, bookstore lady,' came Brett's voice from behind me. He sounded resentful. I tried to ignore him.

Fortunately, Bodin seemed to have grown tired of the conversation and threw the ball at him. 'Come on, Brett. Let's shoot some hoops.'

So I found myself side by side with the person who'd once held a gun to my head. I took a deep breath and willed any feelings of fear away. There were other people within sight and nothing I'd seen in Jeremy since I'd come down to Sydney had made me feel he was likely to hurt me.

He looked weighed down by his load. 'Here,' I said. 'I can carry one.'

'No, it's fine. It's not right to let a lady carry something so heavy.'

His comment sounded forced. I wondered if he was just trying to be nice or if he really did think that way. It was difficult to tell with him.

We reached the door and Angel opened it. As soon as she saw me she let out a string of expletives. 'She's here *again*?'

Jeremy sent her a warning look. 'Angel, what did I say?'

She swore at him and walked out to where the guys were still playing basketball.

'I'm sorry about that,' Jeremy said when she was gone.

'It's all right. If I'm going to be a social worker, I'd better get used to it.'

He raised his eyebrows. 'You're studying social work?'

I sighed. 'I am. Well, I'm trying to, anyway.'

'What do you mean?'

'Not sure I'm cut out for it. In fact, someone I know has told me point blank that I shouldn't do it.'

He shrugged. 'Don't let them get to you. If you want to do it, I'm sure you can.'

I was sure he was just being nice. He didn't know me so was in no position to draw conclusions like that. He was probably just overcompensating for what had happened.

I turned my thoughts to more positive things. 'I hope Rory likes his books.'

His face fell. 'I'm afraid he's not here today.'

I felt a surge of disappointment. 'Oh. I was so looking forward to him seeing them. Maybe I should keep them until he's back. When do you think it will be? Tomorrow? A couple of days?'

Jeremy's eyes darted away from mine. 'I'm not sure.'

There was something wrong. 'What's happened?'

We'd reached the auditorium by that stage and I could see that Jeremy was reluctant to say, but I wasn't going to let up. He must have realised he needed to tell me. 'Can I put these books down first? They're really heavy.'

He took the bags over to Rory's corner and I took them out and arranged them. He helped me put them on the shelf, looking at each one in turn and sometimes chuckling, although his face looked sad.

After a few minutes, my patience was at an end. 'Please tell me what happened.'

Jeremy sighed. 'Jacinta took Rory home last night, like she usually does. His cousin was there and she seemed fine.'

'And?'

'We got a call from her early this morning. Apparently Rory had a fall last night.'

I'd heard a lot about falls during my time in the domestic violence unit.

Jeremy could obviously see my scepticism. 'Yeah, we thought that too. Jacinta went around straight way and he was unconscious. He'd had a blow to his head.'

'Do you know what with?'

'It's difficult to tell at this stage. His cousin said he'd fallen and hit his head on the side of the TV cabinet. Jacinta called an ambulance. She's up at the hospital with him now.'

I was horrified. I sat down on one of Rory's chairs and tried to blink the tears out of my eyes. 'The poor little boy. Will he go to foster care or back to his cousin?'

Jeremy sat cross-legged on the floor. 'There haven't been any other instances bad enough for family services to take him away. He'll go back to her.' He scowled.

'Damn. His life's been so unfair.' I looked around the room at the other kids. 'I guess all of them have a sad story.'

'They do. But that's something they decide to talk about.'

I felt there was a caution in his voice. He was letting me know, nicely, not to ask any of them to tell me their stories.

So what was I there for? There was no Rory and I'd put the books on the shelf for him. 'I don't suppose I could go to the hospital to see him?'

Jeremy shook his head. 'You'd need permission from his cousin to do that. Jacinta's got permission but I don't know if she'd let anyone else.'

I nodded. I was starting to feel more and more awkward. I had no business being there if neither Rory nor Jacinta were. I wasn't exactly a hit with any of the others, in spite of my ability to shoot hoops. 'I should probably go.'

I thought I could detect disappointment in his eyes. 'You don't have to. I mean … I'm sorry, I didn't mean to …' He got up and walked around nervously. 'I'm not trying to make you leave.'

'No, I don't think that. It's okay.' Man, would being around him ever not be uncomfortable?

He stopped his pacing and gave me a nervous grin. 'You could show Bodin some of your basketball skills.'

I appreciated his attempt to lighten things up. 'That's okay. I'd probably better get home. My aunt will be wondering where I am.'

To my surprise, he walked me out. I wondered if I should feel nervous, but we passed some of the kids on our way, so it wasn't like we were alone. Most of the kids ignored me, except Angel, who started her usual diatribe until Jeremy silenced her with a look.

'Don't mind her,' he said. 'She's just not used to …'

He seemed at a loss for how to finish his sentence. I grinned. 'Others of her kind?' It made us sound like aliens. I laughed at the thought. 'It's all right. I don't think she'll have to put up with me much longer.'

'You're going home to Brisbane soon?'

I'd been planning to leave in the next couple of days. After all, I'd done the mediation thing and we both seemed to be doing well as a result of it. The only other thing I'd wanted to do was see Evan. That would hopefully happen the next day. 'I probably should. I need to do some work before I go back to uni. Bank balance is getting a little low.' In reality, my bank balance was okay, but I felt I needed to provide some sort of excuse.

He said nothing but as we arrived at my car and I unlocked it, he reached down and opened the door for me, holding it open until I was inside. While it was embarrassing, I appreciated the gesture. There was no doubt he meant it kindly.

He gave me a nervous smile. 'Thanks for coming. I'm sure Rory will love his books when he gets back. I'll get Jacinta to call you and let you know how he's going. She knows your number, doesn't she?'

'Matt does.'

He nodded. 'And I'll also make sure she gets some of those books to him for you.'

'Thanks. That would be great.'

With that, he stood back from the car and watched until I pulled out of the car park. He gave me a kind of wave and I beeped my horn in reply.

My thoughts were in a whirl as I headed back to Aunt Myrtle's. I was upset about Rory for a start. It was wrong that a child so young should have so much sadness and tragedy in his life.

But my thoughts also lingered on Jeremy. The old image of him in my mind, from the robbery, was disappearing, replaced by a nervous, serious man who seemed to have his own sadness inside him. I was curious about what had caused it but there was no way I was going to ask him about it. I wondered if I could get it out of Jacinta but guessed she'd probably think it was best coming from him. It was a shame, because the desire to know kept rising in me until, by the time I made it home, it was all I could think about.

Chapter Twelve

I'd hoped the old man was right about Evan being home on Fridays. I was still ticked off at him for making it so difficult to find him. It was like he'd washed his hands of me, which might be true. However, I was too concerned about him to do that.

Not to mention that if he found out why I'd come down to Sydney, he wasn't likely to be happy. In fact, he'd probably hit the roof, especially if I let it slip that I'd been back there twice since then.

But I had to see him. I was worried about him. The area he was living in was not good. How had he got there? Did he still have a job? Where? He'd had loads of qualifications. He should have been able to find something that let him live in a decent part of town. I would have thought that was important to him, actually. He'd always seemed to view people from those kinds of neighbourhoods as 'scum' like Jeremy and Cold Eyes.

It didn't help that Jacinta called me during the morning to let me know Rory would probably be in hospital for a few days. So I was feeling unsettled when I pulled once again into the car park at Evan's apartment. This time there were no kids standing around watching me, although I still felt like there were eyes on me when I got out of the car. The same old man was clearing the yard as I walked to the door. He nodded as I approached.

'He's here today,' he said.

At least that was something. I gave him a smile and headed into the lift, where I prayed a lot as it made its rickety way up to Evan's floor.

I took a deep breath as I knocked on his door. Would he be happy to see me? Probably not, since he hadn't told me where he lived. Maybe he was just ashamed of it. I hoped that was the reason.

I had to knock a few times before I got a response. He eventually pulled open the door and I gasped.

It was definitely him but it was hard to believe. His hair was unkempt and he had grown a beard. It looked like he'd been wearing his clothes for a few weeks without changing them.

Could this really be the same guy I'd worked with in Your Corner Bookstore and Café?

I tried to keep the shock off my face but I don't think I did a good job. 'Evan? Hi, it's Maddy. I was in town and I wanted to see how you were.'

He looked me up and down but said nothing. This wasn't going well. 'Can I come in?'

I thought at first he was going to refuse, but he sighed and stepped out of my way. I walked into the apartment and tried to keep my face non-committal as I looked around.

Although I had seen worse, it was not clean. There wasn't much furniture and what was there had clearly seen better days. There were dishes in the sink with things growing on them. I wrinkled my nose at the smell.

Evan pointed to the couch. It was clean compared with other parts of the apartment and he didn't have to clear anything off it before I sat down. He seemed to have recovered from the surprise of seeing me but it was difficult to tell whether he was happy or not. I thought his face seemed a bit brighter than before so I took that as a good sign.

His first words to me suggested I was right. 'It's good to see you,' he said, looking me up and down. 'How did you find me?'

I smiled. 'My aunt rang Michael, who rang your brother.'

He nodded. 'That would do it.'

I didn't see any point in wasting time with talk about the weather. 'Why didn't you tell me where you were, Evan? I was worried about you.'

He shrugged. 'This isn't exactly the Marriott. You shouldn't have come here. This neighbourhood's not great, you know.'

'I noticed that.'

'Did anyone bother you?' I didn't like the way his hands clenched.

'No. It was fine. The guy who works downstairs seems nice.'

He nodded. 'Mr Johnson. He's a good man.'

'And you could have still told me where you were.' I tried not to sound too harsh.

'I know. It's just difficult …' He looked around.

'Why are you here? You couldn't afford anywhere else to live?'

He looked ashamed. 'Money's hard to come by.'

'I thought you were working for a few different places.'

'They didn't work out.'

Surely someone with his skills could have found work? Even back in a bookshop. Then I remembered why I would never work in a bookstore again. 'I'm just glad you're okay. I was afraid something had happened to you.'

He seemed to appreciate that. 'Can I get you a coffee?'

I wasn't sure he'd have any clean cups but I hoped for the best. 'That would be nice.'

Fortunately, he had a stack of mugs that looked new. There was only instant coffee but I could deal with that.

He gave me my coffee and sat down. 'So what have you been up to? Still studying social work?'

'Yeah, I am.'

He must have heard the doubt in my voice. 'You not enjoying it?'

This time I was determined not to sugar-coat it. 'It's difficult dealing with a lot of people who are going through really bad stuff.'

'Maybe you'd be better in another area. Is there something you can do that will get crims caught? You could help battered women go after their husbands, make them pay for what they've done.'

I tried to laugh. 'I'm not sure I'd be good at that either and I don't think social work covers that anyway. It's more about supporting the victims than going after the perpetrators. I think police and lawyers are for that kind of thing.'

He shrugged. 'Others can do it too, you know.'

I didn't like how he said that. 'Like who?'

He leant back in his chair. 'There are people who will bring others to justice when the courts don't do a good enough job.'

I scowled. 'You're not talking about some kind of vigilante, are you? You think we should hire vigilantes to take revenge on people? How is that different from what the criminals themselves have done?'

He glared at me. 'Of course it's different. Did we ask for what happened to us? No. We were perfectly happy minding our own business and not hurting anyone. Two men decided to change that.'

'One of them died and the other went to jail!'

'What, for two or three years?' he scoffed. 'You know that's not enough. You and I, we got a life sentence. We'll never get back to what we were before this.'

I was suddenly overwhelmed with pity for him. He looked like a wreck. What we'd been though *was* ruining him.

Why hadn't that happened to me? Was it because I had a different personality or because I'd tried to deal with it differently? Was it something else entirely?

I tried to soften my voice. 'Evan, you have to see that that's not the answer. Swapping violence for violence, is that really going to do any good, even if we get someone else to do it for us?'

He didn't back down. 'If it gets rid of the evil in our society, then yes, it is.'

I started to get angry. 'And is a person doing that kind of work going to be some upstanding citizen? Are they really any better than the perpetrator of the original crime?'

'Of course they're different!' Evan yelled.

I shrank back in my chair. He'd never yelled at me like that before, with a light in his eyes that made fear creep up my spine.

He must have noticed the fear in my expression because he backed down a little. 'Come on, Maddy. It's not as bad as that. Surely you can see that.'

'I'm sorry. I can't.' Then a cold hand of fear grasped my heart. He was talking like he'd seriously considered this. Was this the real reason he lived not far from where Jeremy worked? Was he planning to send somebody around to deal with him? Would he do it himself? What if he did? Would they only target Jeremy or would some of the kids at the church be caught in the crossfire? That couldn't happen!

It was a question I had to ask. I tried to keep calm. 'Evan, you wouldn't do something like that … I mean, you wouldn't target …'

His answering look was cold. I was sure I had my answer.

'How is that going to solve anything?'

'It will solve plenty.'

He was really starting to scare me. I got up, wondering if I should warn Jeremy so he could go away somewhere and be safe. I looked towards the door.

Evan must have realised I was feeling afraid because he lowered his voice again. He came up to me and took hold of my hands. 'Maddy, please know that whatever happens, it *will* help us.'

I snatched my hands away. 'If you do this, you're not doing it for me. I'm going fine without it.'

'What, with a bout of forgiveness? Believe he's changed? He won't have changed, Maddy.'

'But he has!'

It took me a moment to realise what I'd said. The realisation came to Evan's face a moment later.

He took my wrists this time and his grip was not light. 'You mean you've actually gone to *see* him? Didn't I say not to do that?

You know he'll only lie to you! That's what those kinds of people do. He's lied to that preacher, he's lied to everyone. He's a liar and a thief. You can't trust him!'

I tried to pull my hands away. 'You don't know that. You haven't even met him. You don't want to believe he might not be as bad as you think. You just want to see him as evil so you don't have to change!'

A stinging slap slammed across my face. It was so hard it made my ears ring. I fell to my knees, too shocked to realise straight away what had happened. Then I raised a shaking hand to the side of my face. I could taste blood in my mouth.

I looked up at Evan. He was looking down on me, a horrified expression on his face. A second later, he was on his knees beside me, holding me close.

'Maddy, Maddy, I'm so sorry. I didn't mean to hurt you. I just … you made me so mad. You aren't thinking straight.'

I could feel the tears coming. It was a common thing for an abuser to do—blame his victim for the abuse. I began to cry and he kept holding me but I knew I needed to leave. I got to my feet and backed away.

Once he realised what I was planning to do he tried to apologise, staying on his knees. 'Maddy, no. Please. I didn't mean it. It won't happen again.'

They always said that.

With a sob, I grabbed my bag and wrenched open the door, slamming it behind me. At first I was terrified he would follow me but he didn't. My legs were shaking so much I probably couldn't have run away if he had tried to come after me.

I couldn't remember going down in the lift. I was relieved that the man in the front garden wasn't there on my way out. Nor was anyone else. I raced to my car and locked myself in.

Once there, the tears came in a surge, pouring down my cheeks. I'm not sure how long I stayed there, sobbing, before I turned the rear-view mirror down to look at my face. The right side of it was red and swollen. That caused another stream of tears. My head was aching. I wondered if I'd be able to drive. I probably needed to ice it. Did I need a doctor?

I thought of Jacinta. The church was five minutes away. Although she would probably ask questions about what had happened to me and I wasn't sure I wanted to tell her.

I glanced nervously back at Evan's apartment block. I was still worried he might come after me, even though there was no sign of that.

I tried to calm myself as I started the car. It was hard. Harder still was to keep my mind on my driving. It was difficult to concentrate with my head throbbing so badly.

When I arrived at the church I could see no one. I wasn't sure if that was good or bad. It would have been good if Jacinta was in sight or maybe Pastor Matt.

The only thing I could think of doing was going up and knocking on the door.

Please, please, let Jacinta answer. What would I do if it was Angel?

The door swung open and it wasn't Angel or Jacinta. It was Jeremy.

He took one look at my face and his eyes opened wide. 'Maddy? What happened?'

His shock made me start shaking again. He stepped back so I could come inside and he shut the door behind me. 'Nothing. I need to see Jacinta. Is she here?'

Now the initial shock had worn off, I could see something else on his face. It was anger. He grabbed my wrists the same way Evan had.

'Who did this to you?' he demanded. 'Was it Angel? Did she hit you? Was it one of the others? Damn it, if they did I'll—'

His voice had increased in volume as he spoke until I shrank away. This man looked more like the one I feared, although I wasn't sure who that was now. Was it him or Evan? It didn't seem to matter.

I pulled back on my hands and managed to break free of his grip, crouching on the floor with my hands over my head, sobbing. 'Don't touch me! Don't hurt me, please!'

I heard an intake of breath but couldn't bring myself to look at him. 'I'm so sorry. I shouldn't have …' He didn't seem able to finish. 'I'll get Jacinta.'

He bolted away.

I sat there sobbing for a few minutes before I heard the sound of an approach. Then Jacinta put gentle hands on my arms and pushed them away from my face.

'Maddy, what happened?' As she peered down at me I could see Jeremy looking over her shoulder. She gaped in shock at my face. 'Who did this?' She turned to Jeremy. 'You didn't—'

His eyes were wild. 'Of *course* I didn't! I wouldn't—' He didn't seem to be able to get anything else out. His look became anguished and a strangled sob came from his throat before he ran off.

Jacinta watched his retreat before turning back to me. 'Come on, let's get you some ice.'

She didn't take me to the main hall; she took me to Matt's office. He gave a start of shock when we came in but after a few whispered words from her, he hurried out. He returned a few minutes later with an ice pack before disappearing again. I felt guilty for kicking him out of his office.

Jacinta tended my bruises without saying anything. Gradually my sobs receded and I sat in a chair, my mind in turmoil.

Jacinta said nothing. I was expecting some kind of comment from her, especially if she thought Jeremy was responsible for this. That she would suspect him made me feel awful. 'Jeremy didn't do this.'

'I know. I know him pretty well. I can't imagine him ever doing something like this.'

'He has before,' I spat, remembering how he'd once thrown me to the floor.

She met my eye. 'That was years ago when he was young and bitter and under the influence of another man. Now he's in control of himself. He knows how to curb his anger. He knows how to direct this kind of thing into constructive avenues like his work. He doesn't lash out at anyone unless it's in self-defence.'

'You didn't think that before.'

She sighed. 'I know. I shouldn't have doubted him like that but when I saw you cowering away from him I jumped to the wrong conclusion. I'll apologise to him later.'

I tried to consider what she was telling me about Jeremy but it was hard to think about anything other than Evan.

'So who did this?' she asked calmly.

'Does it matter?'

Her silence spoke volumes. I knew she wouldn't come right out and say I should press charges but I could tell she was thinking it. Or maybe it was just because those thoughts were rattling around inside my head.

'He didn't mean it.' It was so weird to be saying this. How many times in the past year had I heard abused women saying that? Now here I was, trying not to get the man who'd hit me into trouble.

But it was different. This was Evan.

She sat down and looked at me. 'Do you think that maybe Evan needs help?'

'How do you know it was Evan?'

She shrugged. 'You said when I called the other day that you were going to see him and I don't think there are any other people you know down here. And if this was done by some stranger you wouldn't be hesitating to tell me. It has to be someone you know. He's the logical choice.'

I groaned. 'So you think I should report him?'

'I'm not saying that.'

'No, you don't want me to feel forced into doing anything, do you? You want me to feel I'm in control of the situation. We're not supposed to convince the victim to do anything, but that doesn't mean you don't hope I'm going to do it.' I knew that from what little experience I'd had. How often had I sat there wishing I could force a DV victim to make a formal accusation against an abuser? But we weren't supposed to do that as it made us as controlling as the abusers themselves. 'And what good will it do? Going to jail isn't going to help him.'

'I doubt he'd go to jail unless he's got a record when it comes to things like this. More likely he'd get anger management classes or therapy.'

'He's already had therapy.'

Her look was non-committal but the doubts entered my head anyway. Did I really think Evan had had enough therapy to help him? Evan had been proud from the outset and didn't seem to want to acknowledge he needed help. And since I'd known him, he'd seemed to be getting progressively worse in dealing with all this.

How much did I really know Evan? I'd worked with him for a few weeks before the robbery but we'd never even dated or anything back then. It had been a working relationship with a cute, distracting guy. Everything between us had happened afterwards. And what had happened between us? We'd seen each other a few times and phoned and chatted on Facebook. Always about what had happened. Was there anything else we'd ever talked about?

If Jacinta noticed I was coming to that conclusion, she said nothing. She just let me work through it. She was right. If Evan was capable of doing this to me, then he would be capable of doing it to someone else. He needed help.

But it was difficult to do that. Could I really turn in a friend, even if it was unlikely he'd end up in jail? I cringed at the thought. 'I'll go see him again.'

She shook her head. 'That's not a good idea.'

'No, seriously. I think I need to. He was upset with what he'd done. I don't think he'd be in a hurry to do it again.'

'Oh, Maddy.'

It was easy to see how worried she was and I understood why. 'I can't just report him and they go and pick him up.' No, I was sure Evan would be on his guard against doing something like that again. He would know I was within my rights to report him. I felt he would appreciate it if I gave him the option.

She sighed. 'Would you like me to go with you?'

'No. I'll wait a few days but I'll go by myself. I don't want him to feel threatened.'

She seemed frustrated but I knew she wouldn't try to dissuade me. I was sure she'd heard it all before. The annoying thing was, so had I, and I was still determined to do this. It's amazing how objectivity flew out the window as soon as things became personal. I knew I should report Evan but I couldn't bring myself to without giving him a chance.

When the swelling had gone down a bit I knew I needed to go. I wondered what Aunt Myrtle would say when she saw my face.

Jacinta let me go without another word. That was where she was different from Melanie. Mel would have probably called the police herself and made me report Evan. Jacinta was too professional for that.

I felt guilty about Jeremy too. The poor guy. It was terrible that she'd blamed him at first. I flinched every time I remembered the look on his face as she'd said it. Hopefully I could make it up to him next time.

Chapter Thirteen

Aunt Myrtle was shocked when she saw me and wouldn't rest until I told her what had happened. Once she knew, her face grew sadder than I'd ever seen it.

'That poor boy,' she said with a sigh. 'I know how you feel. He *is* good. Or was, at least. The man I met at the bookshop would never have struck you.'

I sat down to eat the dinner she had ready for me. 'Well, that man's gone now.'

She nodded thoughtfully. 'What will you do?'

I pushed the tofu around on the plate. Why Aunt Myrtle liked the stuff I had no idea. 'Jacinta—one of the workers at the church—she thinks I should report him.'

Aunt Myrtle's mouth turned down. 'I understand why, although it seems a shame.'

I nodded. 'What if he does it to someone else?'

'Exactly. Will you do it?'

I shuffled uncomfortably. 'I want to see him again first.'

Her eyes widened. 'Is that wise?'

That was the question. 'I think what he did will make him careful around me, at least for a while. It might give me the chance to convince him he needs to get help.'

'Are you going back tomorrow?'

I shook my head. 'I'll give it a couple of days.'

'I think that's a wise idea.' She put her arm around me. 'Poor dear. You've been through so much. It takes courage to do what you've done in coming down here and it'll take courage to go back and see Evan again. You're a good girl and I know your parents are proud of you.'

It was nice hearing that. It gave me some hope that what I was doing was the right thing.

***

For the next couple of days I didn't do much at all. I didn't feel like going back to the church while my face was so swollen. It was embarrassing. What if the kids asked me what had happened? What would I tell them? I didn't want the questions I knew it would raise. So I stayed at Aunt Myrtle's place and didn't do much more than surf the internet and text Elaine and Crimson and try to avoid sending anything to Mel. I was sure she'd be able to see through the phone and know what Evan had done to me and I knew what her reaction would be.

I also had to push back my departure date. I told my parents I was catching up with Evan and some other people and I needed a bit more time. I decided I'd better not book a return flight until I'd figured out what I was going to do. I didn't want to have to change it again.

It was three days after Evan had hit me when I gathered up my courage and went to see him. My heart was in my mouth as I pulled up in the car park near his building. Once again, no one was around, not even the man tending the garden.

But as I walked up to the building, I thought I saw movement to one side of it. I could see someone standing in the shadows. My heart leapt into my mouth and I hurried to the apartment building, hoping whoever was there wasn't hostile.

I made it inside with no problem and then went back to being nervous about seeing Evan. At least it distracted me from yet another ride in the old lift.

I took deep breaths as I approached Evan's door. Would he be home? How would he react to me being there?

I knocked. No answer. I knocked again. Still no answer. Damn. Now it looked like he wasn't home anyway.

'He's gone,' came a voice from behind me.

I whipped my head around. Standing in the corridor was the old man who worked in the garden. He had a broom and looked like he was sweeping the place, or trying to, anyway.

Once I had recovered from my fright I focussed on what he'd said. 'He's gone out?'

'No. He left. Packed and up cleared out. Just yesterday. Seemed in a hurry to leave. Didn't he let you know?'

My heart sank. 'You mean he's moved away? Did he leave a forwarding address?'

The man shrugged. 'No idea. It's not like we've got an office. Maybe he did with the post office. I don't know.'

Why would Evan do that? I was pretty sure I was the reason. If that was the case, I doubted his brother would tell me where he'd gone … if he knew.

Perhaps the man was wrong. 'Are you sure?'

He nodded. 'Yep.'

He produced a ring of keys and unlocked the door. I was amazed at the emptiness. Most of the furniture was gone, not that he'd had a lot to begin with. There was still mess around, so he hadn't bothered to clean. But he'd taken enough to make it clear he wasn't planning to come back anytime soon.

I couldn't help Evan now. He clearly didn't want to be helped.

I managed to stutter out my thanks to the old man before going back downstairs and walking out of the building towards my car. My heart was heavy. What could I do now?

As I passed the edge of the building I again saw that shadowy figure I'd seen earlier. I jumped with fright. He was nearer now, only a few feet from me. I'd seen him look around as I'd come out.

I stopped in fear, watching him. As soon as he realised I was looking, he turned away, but as I started to back away he looked back. Then he pushed the hood he was wearing down and came towards me.

I started in shock. 'Jeremy?' My heart began to beat faster. 'What are you doing here?' Should I be afraid? An old instinct wanted to fear him.

But the look on his face was not threatening, it was pleading. 'Maddy, it's all right. I'm not going to hurt you. Please, you've got to believe me.'

I was too heartsick over Evan to stay afraid of him, especially with that look on his face. 'It's okay. I do.'

'I'm so sorry. I didn't think about how I would scare you if you saw me here like this.'

It was difficult to care. 'It's all right.'

He looked me over, his glance penetrating. 'Are *you* all right?'

'What?'

He lowered his voice. 'He didn't hurt you, did he? Are you okay?'

Jeremy was here because he was worried Evan would hurt me. The irony was not lost on me and it was that that finally broke me. I burst into tears.

'Maddy? Please don't cry. Are you hurt?'

I shook my head but couldn't get any words out. I couldn't see his face through my tears but his voice sounded lost. 'No. He's gone.'

'What?'

The sobs shook me. 'He's gone. He's moved out. No forwarding address, no nothing.'

He was silent for a moment and when he did speak, he sounded shocked. 'Um … do you want to go back to the church and talk to Jacinta or Matt?'

'Is your car here?'

'No. I walked.'

Continuing to sob, I walked towards my car.

He followed me. 'I really don't think you should be driving. Not while you're crying.'

I held my keys out to him. 'Then you drive.'

I went around to the passenger side without hesitation. Maybe he would kill me or rob me or something worse but I didn't care. I just wanted to cry and not have to think about anything anymore.

He looked uncertain, his eyes darting from me to the keys. 'You want me to drive you?'

'That's the general idea.' I was unable to keep the impatience out of my voice.

He frowned. 'Where do you want to go?'

I rolled my eyes. 'Just drive me wherever. I don't care.'

He made no further debate. I hopped in and barely noticed him starting the car and driving out of the car park.

He didn't say much as we drove, especially since he must have realised I wasn't going to talk back anyway. A couple of times he asked me where I wanted to go but I didn't answer. I just let the tears fall and looked out the window without seeing anything.

I'd missed the chance to see Evan. Would I ever see him again? Would he want me to find him? Everything suggested that he didn't. If that was the case, should I even try?

But I had to. He needed help. He was on a downward spiral and any friend would want to help him out of it. But how did I do that, exactly?

It was then I noticed the car had stopped. I looked around. We were in a car park near a small strip of shops. I looked over at Jeremy and frowned.

He was unbuckling his seat belt. 'Come on, let's go and get some coffee.'

I scowled but then realised that a coffee might be nice. Maybe it would help me think of how I could help Evan.

Before I knew what was happening, Jeremy was beside my door and opening it for me. It was a nice gesture. 'Thank you.'

We walked side by side over to the coffee shop. It was strange to be going for coffee with him. I wondered what Melanie would say if she knew what I was doing, not to mention Elaine and Crimson. I got the feeling my parents would approve, especially if it helped me recover. I had no doubt what Evan would say.

We didn't say anything as we ordered. Jeremy didn't offer to pay for me. I wondered if he had much money. As far as I knew, he only worked at the church and I didn't think they paid much. He didn't pull out my chair at the table either, but I didn't know if that was because there were so many people around us now or if I was too quick and he didn't have the chance.

Sitting with him at a table, just the two of us, was surreal. I was hesitant to meet his eye and in the few times I looked his way, he seemed to be avoiding looking at me.

At least this situation distracted me from thinking about Evan.

'My guess is he's afraid.'

I looked up a Jeremy. 'What?'

'Your friend. I think he's run because he's afraid.'

I reflected on that. 'What's he afraid of, exactly?'

'You. You knowing me. I don't know him. I only met him once and that wasn't in a great circumstance but this whole thing,' he gestured between the two of us, 'would have to be confronting, especially if he doesn't want to forgive me.'

He'd hit the nail right on the head. Not that it would be difficult to figure out. 'Pastor Matt told you he wasn't interested in seeing you?'

He nodded. 'Yeah. I wasn't surprised. I didn't expect either of you to have any interest in seeing me. Especially not you.'

'Why?'

He hesitated before he answered. When he did, his voice was low. 'It was worse for you, especially … with Jack.'

Jack? I could feel my face paling as I realised who he meant. Cold Eyes.

He was watching me carefully. 'Jack ... he wasn't a great guy. But I'm sure you've guessed that.'

I couldn't stop myself from saying it. 'Neither were you at the time.'

'No, that's true. But whether you want to believe it or not, I was telling the truth when I said it was his idea. It was. I know it's no excuse, but I was just a kid trying to hurt someone who didn't care anyway.'

That caught my interest? 'Who?'

He seemed reluctant to tell me. 'My mother.' His face hardened as he said that. 'I don't want to bore you with my family history. I know it doesn't make what I did okay.'

I didn't know anything about his mother and he was right—it wouldn't make what he'd done okay, but I wanted to know. 'You can tell me if you want. I don't mind hearing.'

He gave me a long look. 'You sure?'

I was nervous about hearing it but I wanted to, before I lost my nerve. 'Just tell me,' I snapped, before adding, 'if you're okay with telling me.'

Again, he looked at me for a long time before he spoke. I couldn't work out what was going on in his head. Whatever it was, he put it aside and began to tell his story.

'I'm sure most of it won't be anything new. You've probably heard far worse stories than mine. I've heard far worse. But that doesn't help when you're going through it.

'My mum was a drug addict and she became a hooker to support her habit. My father was one of her clients. She didn't know who. She didn't care. I don't think he was a regular, as she tried to keep guys who had some money as regulars and if she'd thought my father was one of them, she probably would have tried to get some support out of him. It was hard for her to keep guys like that, though, especially as her addiction got worse. In the beginning, she was more a high-end girl. She was really pretty then and there was nothing she wouldn't do. That didn't change.' He rolled his eyes. 'But it wasn't long before her beauty faded, what with all her using.

'Still, because she was up for anything she usually had work until the addiction started to wear her down. By then, I was going to school … when I could, anyway. I went to a local one, which wasn't much, but it taught me to read and write. The school knew about my circumstances so they gave me a uniform and tried to help me out with school books and stuff but it became more difficult as time went on and Mum started to run out of money for drugs. Anything of mine she could find she would hock. I took to hiding things at a friend's place, or anywhere really, so she couldn't get her hands on them.

'You see, I wanted to keep going to school. I didn't want to be like her. I hated her. I know a lot of kids in those kinds of situations get dragged into it themselves but I didn't want anything to do with it. She didn't want me using either, especially as I got older; it would have meant I could steal her drugs for myself and she didn't want that. She told me from the first that the drugs were hers and I was to have nothing to do with them. And that didn't make me want them, especially when I saw what it did to her.

'So I'm this kid who wants to make something of his life in spite of the fact he's got a deadbeat for a mother and no dad at all. I guess the odds were against me all the way. I tried to keep going to school but in our neighbourhood, gangs were something you had to be involved in just to walk down the street. Even then, I tried to avoid them. Ended up getting beaten up pretty bad a couple of times.

'It was when one gang took a knife to me that I knew I couldn't do it anymore. The hospital stitched me up and I came home with this huge scar and my mother was passed out in the lounge room. Even when she came to she didn't notice anything. She just asked me for money. I joined a gang then so people would stop messing with me.

'The gang I joined wasn't huge on fighting but they did a lot of petty crime and all members were expected to participate, so

I did. I stole a lot of stuff. I got good at breaking into places the others couldn't get into, mainly because I was thin. I think it was the main reason they kept me around because I was a dud member in a lot of other ways. I wanted to keep going to school. I still had this idea I could get out of the neighbourhood. But it didn't happen, not in time, anyway.

'Jack Farmer appeared about then. He wasn't part of the gang, or any gang I knew of, but people knew not to mess with him. He'd taken down a few guys in the neighbourhood just for looking at him wrong. But he liked me, maybe for the same reason the others in the gang did. He wanted us to team up. Said I could get a lot of money out of it. By then, all I wanted to do was find my own place and leave the gang. He said there would be no gang; it would just be the two of us.

'He had me do some of the usual jobs but I think he had bigger targets in mind. It wasn't until after I'd joined him that I found out he had a drug habit too. He was also a dealer. I didn't like that at all, but once you'd joined Jack it wasn't like you could walk away from him.

'I'd only been with him for a few months when he suggested that hitting stores was better than break and enters. We'd get more that way. He didn't want to try a bank or anything. Said they had too much security, although I wouldn't have been surprised if he'd tried to do that in the end. He was like that.

'He said it would be easy. But it all went to hell. And so did Jack.'

He fell silent then, his eyes dropping to his coffee cup. I sat in silence as well, processing all that he'd told me. He was right—it wasn't the worst story I'd heard. But I think it was the first time I'd heard of a kid so determined not to sink into those circumstances for as long as he had. I had no idea how hard that would be but I didn't think I'd be able to do it. If that was what you thought life was, why would you even fight it? I had to give him credit for realising that life with his mother was not all there was.

In spite of that, it didn't make a difference. 'A lot of people went to hell that day.'

He rubbed his eyes as if he had a headache. 'You don't know how many times I've wished I could go back and stop it happening. Maybe if I'd found a church like this one, that helps people, they could've stopped me from going that way. But if it wasn't me with Jack that day, it would have been someone else.'

'At least then you wouldn't have to live with it.' I couldn't believe I was empathising with him!

'Yeah, I guess. But I can't change it, can I?'

I nodded. 'That's right. All we can do is move forward.'

He looked at me then, his eyes searching mine. 'You're amazing.' The words seemed to almost force their way out of him and then he seemed ashamed of having said them.

I knew he was referring to my coming to see him but I tried to lighten things up a little. 'I'm *so* not.'

'Not everyone would do what you did.' His eyes were on the table again before he raised them to mine, a serious look on his face. 'I want you to know how much I appreciate it.'

I was getting embarrassed. 'I think you've already said that.'

He leant forward. For a moment I thought he was going to take my hand but he didn't. 'No, I really mean it. You can never understand how much it means to someone like me that you would do that. Obviously it's not something that everyone can do or even wants to do.'

I guessed his thoughts had turned back to Evan. 'Don't blame Evan. He's got loads of stuff to deal with.'

He let out a humourless chuckle. 'Oh, I don't blame him at all.'

'Yeah, I know you don't.' My frustration started to bite. 'You know, I do. Just a little.' I was ashamed to confess it. 'I could have done with someone to hold my hand through it all. I guess maybe I was too hard on him.' I could feel tears gathering in my eyes and I blinked them away. 'I shouldn't have asked so much.'

'Whatever his problem with you, that doesn't mean he can hit you.'

I sighed. 'I know that. I know I should report him but I'm not sure what I should do now he's gone. I don't want him to stay out there without getting help. I guess if I do report him maybe the police can find him.'

His eyes narrowed. 'I wonder ...'

'What?'

He met my gaze. 'Maybe we could find him. I know a few people. I might be able to call in some favours.'

I sat up straight in shock. 'Jeremy, I don't think that's the right way to go about this.'

He looked surprised. 'Why not, if it finds him?'

That flustered me. 'You know that those kinds of people always want favours back. At least, they do on TV.' My ignorance was embarrassing. 'You can't go and ask them to find Evan. What if they hurt him?'

He looked at me uncomprehendingly for a moment. Then his eyes darkened with realisation. He looked disappointed. 'Maddy, I'm not going to ask any gang members or anyone from the old neighbourhood. Not directly, anyway. I meant that I know a few people who work with people on the street. I could ask if they've seen someone. I guess a couple of them might ask someone who's not exactly squeaky clean but I'm not intending to go and ask any favours from any underworld figures. I'm not that stupid.'

He seemed offended and I blushed at how quickly I thought he would only have contacts amongst criminals. That was unfair. 'Sorry. I shouldn't have assumed—'

He instantly looked contrite. 'It's all right. I understand why you would think that, but believe me, I'm careful about who I get involved with. Sometimes I might have to contact someone like that, but I would only do it if one of the kids needed help or something and I sure wouldn't be asking for favours.'

I nodded and waited for the blush to fade from my cheeks. 'Thanks for the offer. Anything you could find out would be great. I'll ask his family, but I've got the feeling he won't tell them, especially if he thinks I'll be asking them.'

We'd finished our coffees by then and I wondered what I should do now. I was feeling better so there was no reason I couldn't drive home. 'I should probably get going. Would you like me to drop you back at the church?'

He nodded. 'That would be great.'

When I arrived at the church I was relieved there was no one outside who would witness me dropping him off like this. What would they think?

As he opened his door, he turned to me. 'I'll let you know if I find out anything. Are you going to be coming back to the church anytime soon?'

'Maybe,' I said. 'Have you heard anything more of Rory?'

He nodded. 'He's back with his cousin. Jacinta said she could take you there to see him if you like. It seems he's been asking after you. She's checked with his cousin and it's okay for you to go there.'

'He can't come to the church yet?'

Jeremy snorted. 'He's supposed to be taking it easy for a few days. Frankly, I think it would be less stressful here than it is at his home.'

'I'd like to see him, even if it's just to give him some of those books to read while he's there.'

'I'll get Jacinta to call you and arrange it.'

I smiled. 'That would be great.'

As he got out of the car, something occurred to me. 'Jeremy, how did you know where I was today?'

He grinned guiltily. 'Your aunt was worried about you. She texted Jacinta this morning and gave her Evan's address. Truth is, I saw the text and I couldn't stop myself. I didn't want you going there by yourself.'

I wasn't sure if that was nice or stalkerish.

'I'm sorry,' he said. 'I shouldn't have done that. I should have guessed how it would look; me waiting there like that. And it wasn't my place to do it anyway. It was a dumb idea.'

I sighed. I was tired of him apologising to me. 'It's all right. I'm sure you meant well. Get Jacinta to call me about Rory. And Jeremy?'

He had just turned away and looked back as I called his name.

'You have my permission to get my phone number from Jacinta and call me yourself if you find anything out about Evan.'

His face lit up in an amazing smile. 'Sure. That would be great.'

He waved as I drove away and I managed to wave back while I tried to sort through the chaos in my mind. Would we be able to find Evan? What would I do if we did?

Chapter Fourteen

The house Rory lived in wasn't as run down as some I'd seen in the neighbourhood. That was one good thing about it.

Jacinta led me up the path silently to the front door. Three of the books I had bought him were tucked under my arm. I hoped he liked them. I hadn't wanted to bring any more. What Jeremy had said about his own mother had had an effect on me. What if Rory's cousin decided to hock them to get something for herself? It seemed safer to leave the majority of them at the church.

A woman in her early twenties answered the door. She was dressed in some kind of work uniform; maybe for a supermarket or something. She didn't look at me but gave Jacinta a small smile. 'Hey.'

'Good morning, Leah. This is my friend Madison, the one who Rory is friends with. Can we see him?'

Leah narrowed her eyes. I wondered what she thought of me being introduced as a friend of her cousin's. She didn't seem to like it but it didn't stop her from letting us inside. Then she walked away, presumably to her room, and left us standing in the hallway.

It didn't matter; Jacinta clearly knew her way around. She led us straight to Rory's room. I was happy to see that it was a nice little boy's room. It was painted a faded blue and had some decals of cars and trucks on the wall. There were a few cheap-looking toys lying around, but no books that I could see. Maybe Leah wasn't much of a reader.

In the corner sat Rory, playing with a couple of toys. There was a medical patch on his head, but otherwise he looked fine.

As we came in his face lit up. 'Maddy!' he said delightedly. 'Did you come in to see me? I missed you!' He flung his arms around my waist.

'Hey, kiddo.' I stroked his hair while his arms were around me, then I knelt down so I was at eye level with him. 'Of course I came. I was so sad not seeing you at the church. And look what I brought for you.'

I showed him the books. 'Are these for me? They're new! That's fantastic!' He looked up at me adoringly. 'Would you read me one?'

I laughed and sat in the chair beside him and read a story to him. Jacinta sat quietly beside us all the way through it, a slight smile on her face.

When I was done, Rory looked up at me in delight. 'That was nice. Do I really get to keep these books?'

'Absolutely. I bought them for you, you know.'

He grinned. 'You can keep them at the church. Soon I'll be able to come and read them there. You can read them to me, if you want.'

'I'll probably have to go back to Brisbane soon.'

His face fell. 'Really? Can't you stay down here?'

I didn't like to disappoint him, but … 'I need to get back to school.'

He put his arms around me. 'I hope you'll come back and see us sometime. I'll miss you.'

'Maybe I will.'

He hugged me tighter. 'I hope so. I don't want you to go at all.'

I think my heart broke just a little bit.

***

I felt guilty as I left because I wasn't sure I'd ever return but I couldn't find it in me to tell Rory so.

Jacinta seemed to agree. 'Are you intending to come back?'

I shrugged. 'I don't know.'

'Then you probably shouldn't have said that. Don't make promises you can't keep.'

I scowled. 'I couldn't tell him I'd never be back.'

Her eyes narrowed. 'Why not?'

'I don't know. It was too hard.' That thought made me depressed. I knew she was right; I shouldn't have given him false hope. I knew I needed to learn to deal with things harder than this if I was going to be a social worker. Did I need any more confirmation that I was too much of a marshmallow for this line of work? 'Maybe Mel was right.'

She raised her eyebrows in an unspoken question.

'My friend Mel in Brisbane,' I explained. 'She thinks I'm not cut out for social work.'

Jacinta smiled. 'You know, I find your take on all this refreshing. That might be just because you're still enthusiastic because it's so new.'

I nodded. 'Yep. Mel says it won't take long before the honeymoon period wears off and I hate every minute of it.'

'I disagree with her.'

I wondered what Mel would say to that. 'Why?'

'Maddy, I don't know you that well, but a couple of things I have worked out about you. Number one, it's in your nature to think the best of everything. Believe me, you need that in this job. You've also managed to stay optimistic in spite of some bad things coming your way. And that's the other thing. In the time I've gotten to know you, do you know what I've seen?'

'What?'

'That you don't give up easily. That will help you in this job. You'll always have to push through moments when you think the kids or whoever can't be helped and they can't ever change. You won't settle for that. You'll keep fighting until you see the light at the end of the tunnel. So no, I don't agree with your friend. I think this job needs people like you. But I know it won't be easy.'

'Believe me, I've worked that out myself.'

***

I was just finishing a Skype session with Elaine and Crimson when I heard Aunt Myrtle's singsong voice calling. 'Maddy? It's time for dinner. Leave the computer. You'll wear out your eyes.'

I tried not to look too tired when I went down for dinner, sure that Aunt Myrtle would blame my exhaustion on the internet.

Aunt Myrtle didn't say much as we ate, at first, anyway. She had been subdued a lot lately. She'd listened to my explanation on why I still needed to find Evan and had accepted my decision not to involve the police. She'd been less happy with the fact that I hadn't told my parents what had happened. She'd only agreed when I promised to tell them when I returned to Brisbane.

Of course, I had no intention of telling them anything and hoped she wouldn't do it herself.

Eventually she broke the silence. 'Do Elaine and Crimson know about your face?'

I rolled my eyes. Aunt Myrtle wasn't one for subtlety. 'Yes, they do.'

She seemed satisfied but then raised an eyebrow. 'I bet your friend Mel doesn't.'

I gave her a sour look. No, I hadn't told Mel. I knew all too well what she'd say about me not calling the police when it came to assault. It wouldn't improve her opinion of Evan by any means.

She took my silence as confirmation. 'I didn't think so.'

'Aunt Myrtle, remember, I am an adult. It's up to me to decide what to do about these things. I'd like you to respect that.'

She pursed her lips. 'I do. I haven't told your parents, have I? But there's maturity and there's willful ignorance, Maddy.'

I was getting annoyed. 'I did tell Elaine and Crimson.'

'Yes, but I don't think they're too likely to try and convince you to do something you don't want to do.'

Boy, was she wrong there. I'd thought that telling them was the safe compromise, but Crimson had hit the roof and threatened to tell my parents herself. I'd told her I would never forgive her if she did. It was the only thing that stopped her. I think it helped when I said I wasn't intending to keep tracking Evan down ... after this time, anyway.

My phone rang and she frowned. 'If that's Evan ...'

I looked down at the phone. It was an unknown number. 'It's probably a telemarketer.'

I left the table and went out the back so I could have some privacy. 'Hello?'

'Um, Maddy?'

It was a male voice I thought I recognised. 'Yes?'

'It's Jeremy.'

In spite of the fact that his call was not entirely unexpected, I nearly dropped the phone. It seemed so odd to be taking a call from the man I'd once been so afraid of. I wondered what Aunt Myrtle would say if she knew I had enlisted Jeremy's help to find Evan.

I pulled myself together quickly. 'Hi, Jeremy. How are you?'

I cringed at the exchange of pleasantries. It sounded so awkward, but he took it in his stride.

'Fine, thanks. I haven't called you at a bad time, have I?'

'No, it's fine. What's up?'

'I just wanted to let you know that I've spoken to a couple of people about finding Evan. Nothing as yet but they seem confident that they should be able to find out something about him.'

'That's good to hear.'

He was silent for a moment and I wondered if I should just thank him and say goodbye, but he didn't give me time. 'You haven't been around here for a couple of days.'

'Oh, sorry. I worried that you might be getting sick of me.' Truth be told, I'd needed the time to try and sort through some things, especially given what Jacinta had told me. Her confidence that I could make a difference with a group like this had filled me with both hope and fear. I'd stayed away deliberately to see how easy it would be to forget about them. It had proved impossible. I'd already decided to go back the next day to put me out of my misery.

'No, we're not sick of you at all. The kids really miss you.'

I chuckled. 'Did they tell you that?' I could imagine Angel moping around and asking after me ... not!

'Not in so many words. But I can usually tell what's bugging them when they start to act up.'

'They've been acting up because I'm not there?'

'You're an interesting distraction for them. You're different.'

'I'm certainly that.'

'Yeah. They don't often spend time with someone who had a normal childhood. Matt's the only other person they have a lot of contact with who's normal and he's a preacher, so they're always looking for ulterior motives with him. With you, you're just there. And you have reasons not to be. I think that makes them curious.'

'Tell them I'll make sure I pop in tomorrow.'

'They'll like that.'

When I came back to the table I could see curiosity in Aunt Myrtle's eyes. 'Who was that?'

'Not Evan.' I couldn't help my snappy tone.

'I didn't think so.'

I frowned. 'Why?'

She gave me a knowing look. 'Because it's been a long time since you've looked like that when you talk about him.'

'Like what?'

'Oh, I don't know. Like you're talking to someone you're fond of. It's someone at that church, isn't it?'

I could feel my face going red. She was barking up the wrong tree.

'Is it one of the workers?' she persisted.

'Aunt Myrtle, I hate to disappoint you, but I'm not interested in anyone at the church. Not in that way.'

She smirked. 'Of course, dear.'

The rest of the meal was silent. I was too embarrassed to keep denying it, especially as I was sure she wouldn't believe me. I was tempted to tell her I was talking to one of the assailants from the holdup just to see how she reacted but that wouldn't be fair on Jeremy. It wasn't right to keep tarring him with that brush.

***

I was surprised when even Angel welcomed me the following day. Admittedly, she only welcomed me with a grunt but that was better than nothing.

I was also surprised to see another girl there. She seemed to be with Bodin. Maybe Angel's acceptance of me was only because there was someone new for her to target. Not that she did anything to the girl. That was probably because Bodin kept giving her warning glances. As a result, she spent a lot of time in the corner, glowering.

Late in the afternoon, Jacinta asked everyone to help pack the groceries for various families. Everyone groaned but no one refused.

'Where are your usual helpers?' I asked.

'They come when they can,' she said, 'but it's all volunteer and they have other things on today. And it just so happens that we got a large donation from a supermarket last night. People need stuff all the time so I don't see any point in waiting to do it.'

I looked around at the grumbling teenagers. 'You have a willing army.'

She raised her eyebrows at me. 'Do you see anyone refusing?'

'One,' Jeremy butted in. 'Bodin's not here.'

Jacinta rolled her eyes. 'Go hunt him down.'

I gave her a curious glance as Jeremy headed off.

'It's the girlfriend,' she explained. 'Bodin's got other sorts of fun on his mind when she's around.'

I grinned but it faded from my face as I noticed Angel slip out. I nudged Jacinta. 'Where's she going?'

Jacinta swore and raced out of the room. I looked around at the other kids but they seemed to know what they were doing, so I followed her.

She'd disappeared from sight almost as soon as she'd left the room, but I didn't need to see Jacinta to know where she was. I could hear the unmistakeable sounds of a fight.

Angel was screaming at the top of her voice, curse words weaving in and out of the screams. I could hear a male yelling as I turned the corner and was shocked to see Angel on Bodin's back, clawing at his eyes. He was trying to dislodge her by throwing his body against the wall. Every time he did it she screamed and cursed and clawed him some more.

Jacinta was in a corner with Bodin's girlfriend, who was holding her hand to a swollen cheek. Jeremy was trying to stop Bodin throwing himself against the wall while pulling Angel off his shoulders at the same time. Every so often she would stop attacking Bodin and aim a hit or a kick at Jeremy instead.

I stood by, wondering if I could help. I kept looking for an opportunity but there were arms and legs flying everywhere.

Jeremy managed to get his arms around Angel and tried to pull her off Bodin's shoulders.

'Get off me, you creep!' she screamed. 'You child molester! I'll sue you!'

Jeremy had a good grip on her but that didn't stop Angel. As she came down towards him, she thrust her elbow back and connected with his nose. With a yelp of pain, he dropped her and raised his hands to his face. They were soon covered with blood.

Now that Angel was off his shoulders and Jeremy was distracted, Bodin turned on her. He thrust her up against the wall and started punching her in the stomach. Her screams were deafening.

'Bodin! Bodin, stop it! *Stop it!*' I tried to grab him from behind. I thought of jumping on his back, but having seen his reaction when Angel did that, I thought it wouldn't be the best move. I tried to hold his arms but he was far stronger than me. I couldn't stop him pummelling Angel.

Her screams stopped and were replaced by agonising groans. It looked like she was about to lose consciousness.

Suddenly all I could see was Evan. Evan being king hit. Evan lying unconscious. I shrieked at the top of my voice and threw myself between the two of them. I thought Bodin was going to strike me at first but then he stepped back.

It was only then I realised that everybody else had crowded into the corridor to watch the fight. I thought I saw some money change hands.

I looked at Jacinta with Bodin's girl. She got up. 'I'll go and get the first aid kit.'

I raced over to where Angel was groaning on the floor. 'We might need an ambulance.'

'No,' she groaned. 'No hospital. I won't go.'

'You should have thought of that before you decided to backhand someone's girlfriend,' I said without thinking.

I looked at her in alarm as she took in what I'd said. To my surprise, she grinned. 'It's what I do best.'

When the ambulance officers arrived they took her in, although the others they treated onsite. By the time they were leaving Matt had arrived, along with a few others from the church who had heard about the incident.

Matt's face was full of concern. 'Is everyone all right?'

'We're fine,' I said, from where I was holding a cold compress to Jeremy's face. 'There was just a minor disagreement.'

'Mm.' That was all he said. I gathered from his face he was familiar with minor disagreements. I wondered how often this happened.

Jacinta came up then and Matt turned to her for an update. 'I managed to get Angel to go with the paramedic. She wasn't too keen.'

'Have you let her family know?' Matt asked.

She nodded. 'I don't think they care much but they know.'

He knelt over to look at Jeremy's face. 'Are you sure you don't need to go to the hospital?'

Jeremy shook his head. 'She busted my nose but it's not the first time it's happened.'

'You should still get a doctor to look at it.'

He grinned at me. 'Why when I think she just straightened it back up?'

I scowled at that but Jacinta laughed. 'Yeah, she's not going to make it worse than it was. You should have seen it before, Maddy. He could move it around.'

I shuddered. 'Ew!'

'At least it's still on his face.' Having said that, Jacinta turned to Matt. 'I think everything's back to normal now. Jeremy's going to go in to the hospital soon to make sure Angel's not causing too much trouble. So if you guys think you can handle things from here, I have a date I'm late for.'

Matt's face brightened. 'Where's he taking you tonight?'

She smiled as she walked away. 'It's a surprise.'

'Hm, that sounds promising.' Matt rubbed his hands together, looking delighted. He was like a proud dad. Then he turned back to Jeremy. 'I think we'll shut for tonight. Is that okay?'

Jeremy sighed. 'We probably need to.'

I nodded. 'Then I suppose I'd better get going too.'

Matt waved goodbye and went to shut the church as Jeremy took the cold compress from me. 'Thanks for the help. I think I'll be okay from here.'

'You sure?'

'Yep.' He gave me a smile.

I was not in a hurry to go. I had a question and I didn't know how to ask him.

He must have noticed my reluctance. 'You okay?'

I didn't want to hassle him but I knew I'd never get to sleep if I didn't know the answer to this question. 'I know it hasn't been long but I was wondering if you'd heard anything more about Evan yet.'

He shook his head. 'No. Nothing more. I'll let you know when I do.'

I sighed. I'd known that was the likely answer.

'Don't worry about it, Maddy,' he said. 'We'll find him.'

I nodded. I would have to hope he was right. 'See you tomorrow.'

'You're coming here tomorrow?' he called as I headed for the door.

'I may as well,' I replied. 'It'll give me something to do while I wait.'

I didn't turn back to see what his reaction to that was. I wondered what he thought. I had been telling the truth, of course. What else was I going to do in Sydney? The only other people I knew down here were Evan and Aunt Myrtle. I saw Aunt Myrtle every day anyway and I didn't know where Evan was. I may as well spend the day with the kids.

'Besides,' I said to myself on the way home. 'I like working with those kids. It's good practice for my social work studies. Maybe I'll get extra marks.'

And who knew? Maybe when I went back to uni I'd even convince Mel I should be doing this.

Then I realised that it was only another couple of weeks until school started back. My heart sank. Although I'd only originally been going to stay a week, it had already stretched to a few more. It was going to be hard going back, especially if we hadn't found Evan by then. Even without that, there was no denying I'd miss everyone at that church. I'd grown to like the kids, even Angel, with all her challenges. And Jacinta had become a good pal and sounding board. Matt was cool too.

And Jeremy? I didn't want to view him as the villain anymore, although it was surprising how rarely those thoughts entered my head these days. It was becoming easier to view him as a normal person.

Chapter Fifteen

The next morning I was unable to think about anything but the kids at Westside church. I couldn't settle myself into doing anything, even chatting on Skype to Elaine and Crimson. I was uncertain about going there so early in the day. I wasn't even sure what time the kids started turning up. Knowing them, it was probably pretty early, especially since it was a Saturday.

I must have been fidgeting because Aunt Myrtle commented on it. 'Why all this pacing up and down, dear? Something on your mind?'

'No, but there's somewhere I need to be. Can I borrow the car again?'

She laughed. 'Of course. I don't use it much. It's a good thing I didn't sell it last year like I was going to.'

I gave her a quick goodbye. If I was so unsettled that I was bothering Aunt Myrtle I may as well put myself out of my misery and go to the church, even if I was earlier than usual.

As I drove, I looked at the neighbourhood around me. I could remember when I'd first gone to the church, how I'd looked at the surrounding houses with fear and disdain as I saw how rundown they were. Now my response was different. While I still noticed the problems, I was focussing not on what they told me about the standards of the neighbourhood, but on how to fix them. That house needed a new fence, or at least, someone to fix the old one. That house needed a new footpath. That house's garage door was coming off its hinges. All fixable things. Could a team from the church help with things like that? I'd have to ask Pastor Matt.

When I turned into the church's car park there was no one there. It was past ten by then, so I would have thought some of the kids would be outside playing basketball. Then I noticed it was wet on the ground. There must have been a shower or two. Maybe it had chased them inside.

As I went up to the front door I didn't even bother raising my hand to knock. I remembered well what Angel had told me the second time I'd visited—*what, do you think this is a bank or something?* I almost laughed out loud at the thought. No, it wasn't a bank. I opened the door and went in.

All was quiet in the entryway. I expected to be able to hear somebody in the back, but there were no sounds, although ... was that someone moving around in the main part of the church?

'Hello?' I said as I came around the corner.

I stopped dead in my tracks. I could feel my face paling because there was a gun being pointed straight at it. I probably would have fallen to my knees had not an additional shock forced me to remain on my feet.

The man holding the gun was Evan.

'Evan, what the hell are you doing?' I said.

'You stupid girl!' he yelled. 'What are you doing here? You're going to ruin everything!'

'Maddy,' came an urgent voice.

As I turned I realised that there were other people in the room. Not many—just Pastor Matt and a couple of the younger kids who looked terrified. And standing in front of them, the man who had spoken to me, was Jeremy.

I raced over to him and looked them all over, especially the kids. They seemed all right. I turned back to Evan, my anger mounting. 'Are you crazy?'

Jeremy put out a hand, trying to get my attention, but Evan

didn't like that. He came up to him, waving the gun in his face. 'You stay away from her. You don't touch her, you hear me?'

He backed away from them all, pointing the gun at us before he directed his angry eyes at me. 'You're the crazy one. I told you to stay away. You didn't. Why couldn't you have listened to me for once?'

Filled with rage, I was about to shout back at him when Jeremy caught my eye. He gave a warning shake of his head. It was a risk for him to do that because it turned Evan's attention back to him. 'I said leave her alone!' He held the gun higher.

Matt stepped forward a little, both hands raised. 'Look, we don't want anyone to get hurt. If you just tell us what you want, we can get it for you and we can all go home.'

'I'll tell you what I want,' Evan spat. 'I want *him*.' He gestured at Jeremy.

'You can't be serious!' I looked at Jeremy's grim face. I was sure he would hand himself over if he thought it would get Evan out of there. I couldn't let that happen. 'Think what you're doing.'

'I *am* thinking.' Every word was enunciated, almost as if he thought he was talking to a child. 'I have done nothing but think about this for years. Don't you get it, Maddy? We need justice and it was never done. It needs to be done if we're going to move on from this.'

'*We?*' I shook my head incredulously. 'Evan, I have moved on. That's why I'm here. At least, I had before today. Now you're just putting me right back in the middle of it again!' The horror was crashing down on me. Once more I was facing a man with a gun, only this time it was someone I knew. I wasn't sure if that was better or worse. The look in Evan's eyes was not much different from the other set of eyes I'd feared for so long. Only more wild, more unbalanced.

Some of my words must have got through to Evan because his voice lowered. 'Maddy, it's all right. I'm going to make it okay again.'

'What, by killing someone? Is that what you're going to do? How does that make it right?'

I was spiralling out of control and I knew it. The two kids

with us were sobbing on the floor. Pastor Matt's shielding arms were around them. I knew only too well how they felt. It would take them years to recover from this trauma and it was all Evan's fault. 'How does this make you any different from the last man who pointed a gun at me?'

Evan glared at me. 'Don't you dare say that. I am *not* like them.' He spat at Jeremy.

'Well, who's holding the gun? It's not him.' I turned and jabbed my finger in Jeremy's direction. 'You're the one holding us here. You're the reason these kids are crying on the floor. That's no one else but *you*!'

Out of the corner of my eye I saw Jeremy reach for me. That set Evan off again. He came over to Jeremy and shoved him up against the wall, his arm across Jeremy's throat. He held the gun to his head. 'Don't you touch her. Don't you do anything to her!'

I made a move to go and try and stop him but Pastor Matt grabbed me. 'Don't,' he whispered. 'You'll set him off again.'

I looked back, holding my breath. Jeremy did nothing to defend himself. He regarded Evan seriously but without malice, even as he struggled to draw breath. I had seen enough of Jeremy to know that he stood a reasonable chance of fighting Evan off, but he probably didn't want to take the risk of someone getting shot in the process.

'I'm happy to go with you,' he managed to choke out. 'Let's take this somewhere else so no one gets hurt.'

My heart filled with fear. I couldn't let that happen. Even if Jeremy did try and fight, Evan could still shoot him and kill him, or at least injure him, in the process. And what if Jeremy felt that he deserved whatever Evan did to him? No. I had to stop it.

Evan gestured towards the door with his gun. 'Go on, then. We'll take this elsewhere.'

'No. No!' Before I could stop myself, I stepped between Evan and Jeremy. I stood there, staring Evan down.

He scowled. 'Get out of the way, Maddy.'

I didn't move.

He grit his teeth. 'I said get out of the way.'

'It's all right, Maddy,' came Jeremy's voice from behind me.

'No, it's not,' I said, without turning around.

'Leave her alone,' Evan snarled at Jeremy.

'No, you leave *him* alone!' I screamed, tears forming in my eyes. 'Get out of here and never come back. You're no better than *him*!'

I could tell Evan knew I wasn't referring to Jeremy. His face turned red, then white. 'Don't you *ever*—'

His voice was cut off as someone grabbed his gun arm from behind. It was Pastor Matt. I hadn't noticed him sneaking up behind Evan.

'No!' Jeremy shouted. I was flung to the ground. Or maybe I dived away myself. I couldn't tell. When I picked myself up I saw Pastor Matt and Jeremy fighting on the ground with Evan, both men trying to wrest the gun from his grip. I looked around. The children were gone. Matt must have told them to run when Evan's back was turned.

'Maddy, get out of here!' Jeremy said as they struggled.

But I couldn't move. I was frozen.

I couldn't see the gun from where I was but I knew the men were fighting for it, although Pastor Matt seemed to be backing away, probably realising that Jeremy had a better chance than he did. I wanted to try and stop them myself but I knew there was nothing I could do. I'd probably only make it worse.

I jumped as a shot rang out, clapping my hands over my ears. However, both of the men kept struggling. I didn't know where the bullet had gone but Matt's eyes met mine and I knew he was okay.

Finally, Jeremy pulled Evan's arm straight up and bent his fingers back. Evan screamed in pain. Matt was ready and took the gun as soon as Jeremy had full control of it. He quickly removed the bullets. Then he ran out of the room.

Now that he was disarmed, Evan didn't stop fighting. He

started hitting Jeremy with his fists, screaming abuse at him. But Jeremy was more than capable of dealing with something like that, especially since Evan was hardly in the best physical condition. He pinned him to the ground.

By then, Pastor Matt had returned. 'I've called the police,' he said. 'They should be here soon.'

'Where are the kids?' I demanded.

'They're in the auditorium. They're pretty shaken.'

That was all I needed to hear. The other two could handle Evan. I needed to help those kids.

By the time the police arrived, I'd managed to calm them down. I hadn't really met either of them before that. They were a brother and sister, Hayley and Jake, both nine and ten respectively. They seemed okay when the police were questioning them but I was already anticipating the kind of trauma counselling they'd need to recover from something like this.

By the time I returned to the church area, Evan was being taken away. I could hear him sobbing. He saw me with the kids as they loaded him into a police car. 'Maddy, I'm sorry. I didn't want to do it. I did it for us.'

While I felt sorry for him, I was also furious. I didn't try to stop the feeling. It was a justified response and one I had to work through before I could begin to recover.

Jacinta came up to me. I hadn't seen her arrive. 'You okay?'

'Yeah, I'm fine. It's the kids I'm worried about.' I gestured to the two of them, who were still tucked under my arms.

She held out her arms to them and they stepped into her embrace. 'They'll be okay. We'll make sure of that. But are you sure you are?'

I nodded. 'Don't worry about me.'

I could tell that wasn't going to be enough to appease her but she didn't push it just then. She simply smiled and walked off with the kids.

Jeremy was standing to the side with a cop who was taking his statement. As soon as he was free he came up to me, concern clear on his face. 'Are you okay?'

'Yeah, I'm good.' I took a deep breath. My voice was *not* going to shake. It was harder to hold it together now I didn't have the kids to distract me.

That reply didn't seem to be enough for Jeremy. 'Are you sure? I couldn't believe it … I mean, when you walked in, that you would be back there …'

He seemed on the verge of tears but blinked them back as I put a hand on his arm. 'I'm okay, really. Maybe I'm getting used to it.' I gave a bleak laugh.

He seemed to appreciate my attempt to lighten the situation. 'I hope not.'

I sighed. 'Well, maybe it's just because it was Evan.'

He lowered his eyes. 'You didn't fear him so much.'

'Oh, I was scared of him when he had that gun. But I'm angry at him more than anything else. He did exactly what he hated you for and he traumatised two children in the process. How twisted is that? He knows what those kids would have gone through. We went through it ourselves but it didn't stop him. He just went ahead with it because he thought … I don't know what he thought.'

His voice was reflective. 'I guess he just needed closure.'

I wasn't buying that. 'By imitating what he hated? Yeah, that's going to bring closure.'

'Don't be too hard on him.'

'Well, don't you be so easy on him. This is exactly what I told you about. I'm the one who fought to recover and he took the easy way out and decided to hate. Then he drags me back there with him, pretending he's doing this for me. Give me a break!'

He gave me a steady look. 'Don't hate him either.'

That took the wind from my sails but I wasn't giving up completely. 'It's important to work through your anger before you can move on to forgiveness.'

'Yeah, but don't forget to do the moving on.'

I sighed. 'I know. I think that's what Evan forgot to do.' I sat down in one of the pews. Jeremy sat next to me.

Pastor Matt came up to us. 'You two okay?'

We nodded. 'We're just debriefing.'

Matt sat down and put his head in his hands. 'Man, I didn't know what was going to happen when that gun appeared.'

'When did he arrive?' I asked.

'He came to the door. I didn't know who he was. He said he was looking for you. I thought you'd be coming today so I thought I'd offer him a cuppa and we could chat while he waited for you. I just thought he was a friend. Hayley and Jake turned up at pretty much the same time and Jeremy came through to take them out back, and he recognised Evan. It was then he produced the gun and told us he wanted Jeremy to go with him. I was trying to talk him out of it but he wasn't too responsive.'

'Tell me about it.'

Jeremy scowled at Matt. 'You took a hell of a risk trying to get that gun from him like that.'

Matt grimaced. 'I know, but I had to do something. I'd told the kids to skip out the back while Maddy had him distracted but I was worried he was going to shoot one or both of you. I couldn't let that happen.'

'You're lucky it didn't. That bullet could have hit any one of us.'

I looked around. 'Where'd it go?'

Jeremy nodded to a wall where the police were nosing around. 'It's over there. I think it missed Matt by about a half a metre or so. You were lucky more than anything else.'

Matt grinned. 'I'll chalk it up to divine intervention.'

Just then Jacinta appeared with steaming cups of coffee. 'Here. Get this into you.'

The police came to have a word with Matt. I turned to Jacinta. 'What do you think will happen to Evan?'

'Well, this wasn't just a slap across the face. It probably depends on what he pleads. He would definitely be up for some extensive therapy, at the very least, but jail time's definitely a possibility.'

I thought about that. My anger must have been fading, because I didn't want Evan to go to jail. In fact, I felt weary about the whole thing. Why couldn't it all just go away?

But Evan in jail? Would that do anyone any good? 'At least then he'd have to take the therapy.'

'I'd say so.'

Maybe that was the best thing. If he was forced to seek help he might actually be helped, although probably not unless he acknowledged he needed it.

Jacinta looked at me. 'Do you think you'll go to see him?'

I shuddered at the thought. 'Do you think it would do any good?'

She shrugged. 'It's difficult to say.'

'He didn't seem too responsive to Maddy today,' Jeremy said. 'Although at least he didn't try to hurt her.'

Jacinta nodded. 'That's a good sign. We'll see what happens and go from there.'

***

This time I managed to convince my parents to stay in Brisbane, rather than race down to help me with my recovery. And it didn't prove as bad as last time. Yes, I began jumping at shadows again, but I seemed to be settling quicker. I wasn't sure if that was because it was Evan and I'd just been less scared or because, being the second time, I knew how to deal with it better. It could have been either.

I resolved I would see Evan, though. I wasn't sure if I would be allowed at first, but I was. Maybe Jacinta or Pastor Matt pulled some strings. Maybe they thought seeing me would do him some good. Whatever the reason, I was able to visit. He was being held in jail. Bail had been set, provided he stayed away from Jeremy, but it didn't matter. He couldn't afford to pay it.

He seemed calm enough. I greeted him as normally as I could. 'Hey, Evan.' I didn't bother asking him how he was. That would be dumb.

'Hey.' He seemed embarrassed to look at me. He said nothing more for a while and I could think of nothing to say, so we sat in silence.

Finally, he spoke up. 'Maddy, I'm really sorry for what happened.'

I noticed he didn't say sorry for what he did, so I was wary. But there was no point in calling him out on it. He needed to come to that realisation himself. 'I'm sorry too.' What else could I say?

He sighed and looked down. 'That's the party line, isn't it? You're not going to tell me how wrong I was to do it. It would be right to say that, though. With those kids there and everything.' He shook his head.

This was more promising. In fact, it was more than I'd hoped for.

He looked up at me. 'Are they okay?'

'Physically they are. But they'll need therapy. They'll probably have to deal with PTSD for a while and have a support network around them. You know how it is.'

He lowered his eyes again. 'Yep. I do. Been there. Guess I just have to hope they don't decide they want to kill me for it. Not that I'd blame them.'

That was definitely surprising. Maybe he'd finally realised the full impact of what he'd done. 'I'll make sure they don't go that way. I don't think it will do them any good. I don't … it's difficult to tell at this stage, but I don't see them reacting in that way. They're both … good kids.'

I'd nearly stopped what I was saying but I was sure he'd have guessed what I was going to say anyway. He grimaced. 'Unlike me, you mean?'

My heart filled with compassion. 'That's not true. You were good. I know.'

'I notice you're using the past tense.'

I sighed. I hadn't gone to see him in order to judge him. 'You *are* still good, Evan. You just lost your way. You need to find it again.'

He didn't answer for a long while. But eventually, when he looked back at me, there seemed to be some sort of realisation in his eyes. 'I *am* sorry, you know. You can tell that to the kids. I know it probably won't mean anything to them. You can even tell it to—' But he stopped short of going that far.

Even so, that was still progress. I smiled. 'I will tell them. All of them.' He didn't object to that and he seemed a little more at peace when I left. I hoped it would be the beginning of the road to recovery for him. It was a shame, though, that it had taken such a horrible event to get through to him.

Chapter Sixteen

The week following the incident I was at the church almost constantly, mainly to look after Hayley and Jake. They seemed to be managing okay. We were keeping an eye on them and Jacinta and I both helped wherever we could.

Pastor Matt and Jeremy both seemed to take it okay, although Jeremy was reluctant to talk to me. I didn't want to ask him for an explanation, but one afternoon when it was just him and me I couldn't stand the one word answers from him anymore. 'Look, why don't you just tell me what's up so you can get it off your chest.'

He frowned at me, as if surprised I'd noticed. 'I'm sorry. I shouldn't be … I just still can't believe you did it.'

'What?'

'Threw yourself in front of a gun. Not exactly a smart move unless you want to get shot.'

I knew he had a point. But I had one for him. 'What would you have done if it had been me he was threatening?'

He opened his mouth and closed it again, looking away as he answered, 'That's different.'

'Why? It's fine if a guy does that but not a girl, is that it?'

He scowled. 'That's not what I meant.'

'Yes it is, actually.'

'You took the risk of getting yourself shot.'

'Evan was more likely to hurt you than me.'

'Better me than you!'

I couldn't believe he thought that way. I softened my voice. 'Do you really think I would have been okay if Evan had taken you out of there and left the rest of us? I couldn't let that happen.'

He didn't answer but I knew what he was thinking. 'Don't go there,' I said. 'You're worth saving. I'm sorry if you don't think so but I do. I mean, what would these kids do without you?'

He was silent for a moment before he said, 'That's true.'

I couldn't interpret the expression on his face. 'It *is* true. You're needed here. Don't ever think you aren't.'

That made him smile. I almost gave him a hug but I wasn't sure how he'd deal with it so I stopped myself.

Jacinta burst into the room. That was a surprise; I'd been told she wasn't working that night. Her eyes seemed brighter than usual, as though they were backlit. They met mine and she glanced down shyly. That wasn't like her. What was going on?

Jeremy was also watching her intently. Was there something between them?

Jacinta came towards me. 'Hey.' She said nothing more, although it looked like she was about to.

'What's up?' I asked.

With a flustered look, she raised her left hand to display a bright diamond ring on her finger.

I shot to my feet. 'What is that?' Dumb question; it was pretty obvious what it was.

'I'm getting married!' She looked like she was about to jump up and down in her excitement. Not something I would have expected from Jacinta but I guess engagement rings do that to a person.

Jeremy was suddenly at her side and pulled her into a hug. 'That's fantastic news.'

She stepped back and narrowed her eyes at him. 'I don't think it was news to you though, was it?'

He grinned. 'Tony said he was planning to propose soon.'

By this time the few kids who were with us that day crowded around to see what was happening. Bodin's girlfriend, Alana, was the only female there apart from Jacinta and myself, so most of them lost interest fairly quickly. However, Alana and I gushed enough to satisfy Jacinta.

Matt came in after a while and also gave her a hug. 'I'm so happy for you. Let me know if you want to have the wedding here and it will be done.'

'We wouldn't have it anywhere else, Matt. You know that.'

'Are you going to buy a house?' Alana asked. I guess that meant the ultimate in commitment for her.

Jacinta looked down. 'Tony's a teacher, you know. He hasn't been teaching long and he's going to be transferred to the country sometime in the next twelve months. He's been renting locally, but we're not going to buy around here, not yet, anyway. We'll leave that for when we get back.'

Matt's face fell, although he didn't look all that surprised. Maybe they'd already discussed it. 'When will you leave?'

Jacinta's eyes passed over me. 'Not this year. We'll need to do it next year, though.'

Some of the kids overheard and looked upset by the news. Alana hadn't known her long enough to be that upset, so she simply went on with her questions.

I wondered what they would do without Jacinta. She had a great bond with these kids. I was sure she'd miss them as much as they'd miss her. I'd known she had a boyfriend but I hadn't known it was that serious.

I looked at Jeremy. How would he feel about her going? He didn't seem too worried. He'd started playing pool with Bodin.

When I was about to leave Matt asked me to come to his office. Uncertainly, I sat in one of his chairs while he organised some papers at his desk. He looked nervous. I wondered if there was something wrong.

He didn't seem in a hurry to start a conversation, so I started one myself. 'I guess you'll all miss Jacinta when she goes. She does such a great job here.'

'She does. But we've known for a while that this might happen.'

He cleared his throat nervously. 'Actually, Maddy, that's what I want to talk to you about.'

I frowned. 'Why?'

'I've noticed you've built up a rapport with some of the kids yourself. We've been talking a lot about what you've done since you've been here and you seem happy to be around since you keep coming back all the time?' He looked at me for confirmation.

I realised where this was heading.

'I know you live in Brisbane and you have a year to go in your social work studies but we'd be more than happy to give you a job at the end of that. Jacinta doesn't have to go anywhere for the next year so we could wait until you graduate, if you're interested.'

I was already shaking my head. 'I don't know about that.' I kept coming back to Mel's opinion. Was I really cut out for this kind of work?

'I understand it might be difficult for you but Jeremy has said he'd be happy to do anything to make you feel more comfortable about it. He'll move on if that's what you want.'

I looked up in shock. 'He'd leave? He can't do that just because you want to offer a job to me! He was here first.'

He looked relieved and confused at the same time. 'So he's not why you're reluctant to consider it? I can see you're not sure. I just assumed … We'd already discussed this possibility between the three of us and we were sure that Jeremy's presence would be the only problem.'

It was terrible to hear that Jeremy was prepared to leave a job he clearly loved just because they were going to offer one to me. 'I couldn't do that to him. He can't leave his job just for my sake. That's unfair.'

He cocked his head. 'Is something else wrong, then? Is it the money? I know it's not great but there's not much we can do about that. We're fortunate to have some generous supporters but their help only goes so far.'

I blushed. 'No, it's not the money. I can always stay with my aunt.' There was no doubt in my mind Aunt Myrtle would be fine with that idea.

'Is there something else?'

I sighed. If he was going to be my boss one day, I owed it to him to be honest. 'I'm not sure I'm cut out for this kind of work. Before I came down here I was thinking of quitting. There are a lot of aspects of the job I find difficult to deal with.'

He smiled. 'I don't think any of us has all the answers to this kind of thing. I do know that theory only goes so far. A lot of it is learned on the job, especially since everybody's different.

'We've had some social work students here before and none of them have been the instant hit you have. The kids are fascinated by you because you represent something that only I've told them about before, and that's forgiveness. They thought no one was capable of that in reality until you showed up.'

I shook my head. 'That's not enough to qualify me to work with them.'

'Not on its own, no, but you've done the training and you've stuck with these kids. You haven't backed down even when they've treated you badly. You've earned some respect here. I'm not going to tell you it's going to be plain sailing because it's definitely not, but that won't change no matter how much training you get. And I'd rather take on someone who already knows the kids and who they like than someone who's new and untried.'

Could I really do it? Even though it was bad pay, it sounded like a dream come true. I could leave my studies with a job to walk into. And I liked these kids. I wanted to know what happened to Rory. I wanted a reason to follow up on him. I wanted to play more basketball with

Brett. I wanted to try and get Angel to accept other girls here.

Then there was Jeremy.

I knew there was no reluctance in my mind when it came to the thought of working with him. I'd seen how good he was with the kids and what a great influence he was and I had seen first-hand how controlled he was.

Matt held up his hands. 'I don't need an answer tonight. Just think about it and talk it over with your family. It would be good to know before you go back to Brisbane, though.'

'That's next week.' I'd been trying not to think about it.

His eyebrows rose. 'That soon? I guess it would be. I hadn't realised that January has already been and gone. Can you let us know next week, then? We'd really appreciate it.'

I nodded. 'I'll do that.'

I left his office in a daze. What was I going to do? Should I take this job? Would I actually help anyone or would I just make it worse? I honestly didn't know.

I resolved to do my best to figure it out.

Chapter Seventeen

Aunt Myrtle was busy with her book club when I came home that night so I didn't have a chance to talk to her, but at breakfast the next morning she poured my tea with a thoughtful look on her face.

'What's up, Maddy? Last night you came home with such an enigmatic look. Did something happen to one of the kids?'

'No, nothing like that. Jacinta's getting married.'

She looked puzzled. 'Why would that make you look so uncertain?'

I sighed. 'Her fiancé is a teacher and he'll be going to the country to teach some time in the next year, so Jacinta will be going with him. The church has offered me her job when I've finished my degree.'

Aunt Myrtle seemed stunned. She sat back in her chair with a thud. 'Really? Did you accept it?'

'I said I'd think about it and let them know.'

She took a moment to process that, taking a gentle sip of her tea. 'You could stay here of course, if you want to. You know that.'

'Yes.'

'So accommodation is no problem.'

'It won't pay much.'

'That's true, but it will be good experience.'

I got the feeling she wanted to say more. She was looking thoughtfully at me over the rim of her teacup. I tried prompting her. 'So you think I should take it?'

'That's up to you, but you do seem fond of the place, so I think you'd probably do well there.'

That was true. I was interested in the welfare of the kids and that would help me to work through all the problems that were bound to arise from time to time. It was a good reason to say yes.

I had a Skype session with Elaine and Crimson later and they weren't impressed to hear that I might move to Sydney, especially considering who I'd be working with.

'Are you seriously going to be okay working with the guy from the holdup?' Elaine asked.

'Yeah. He's changed a lot and is really good with the kids.'

A look passed between them. 'Really?' Crimson said, her eyes narrowing. 'That restoration thing must have worked.'

'At least we'll have somewhere to stay when we come down for a visit,' Elaine put in. 'Sydney's much more alive than Brisbane.'

'I'll be living with my aunt, you know. I don't think you're going to get liveliness here.'

'But you won't live there forever, will you, Maddy?'

I rolled my eyes. 'With the salary I'll be getting I don't think I'll have much choice.'

'Maybe you can flat with someone else down there.'

There was suggestion in Elaine's voice. I smirked. 'Any ideas who?'

'Yeah, there's bound to be some cute guy down there who's the real reason you want to stay. We know it's not Evan, not now. At least, not until he gets himself together.'

'He was never good enough for you anyway,' Crimson said. I almost snorted at that. She'd never felt that way about Evan before.

'So is there someone, Maddy?' Elaine asked.

'No.' I was sure of that.

'We'll just have to see what happens.'

Crimson nodded. 'Yep. You never know what's around the corner.'

***

My conversation with Mel was annoying.

'Are you sure you're up for this?' she said once I told her what was happening.

'I'm not sure. That's why I'm still considering it.'

'Maddy, seriously. Just because you've spent some time with these kids doesn't mean you can handle it. You probably haven't seen them at their worst.'

After all I'd heard about Angel, she was probably right. Still, her negative attitude was irritating. 'So you don't think I can do it?'

'You were struggling this year on your placement.'

'That was with battered women!'

'And you're not going to see any of those there? You might see battered kids. That would be worse.'

My blood boiled at her words, especially as I thought of poor little Rory and all he had to put up with. 'And maybe I can deal with it. Maybe I can help them. Just because I haven't been through that myself doesn't mean I can't be there for them.'

I stopped as I remembered I was talking to a woman who had suffered for years at the hands of her abusive husband. 'Mel, I'm sorry. That was insensitive.'

She was silent for a moment. 'No, it's all right.'

'No, really I—'

'Maddy, would you shut up for a moment and listen to me?'

I shut my mouth and prepared for her scolding.

'I liked what you said. I think that's the first time I've ever heard you come out swinging with that kind of conviction. You weren't even that passionate when it came to defending Evan. I thought that might have been because you weren't that strong but maybe it's because you were unsure about him.'

I didn't answer. I didn't want another tirade from her over Evan.

'So maybe you have more spirit than I gave you credit for.'

That sounded promising. 'So you think I can do this?'

She sighed. 'Maybe. We'll see. I'll have to see you face to face before I know for sure. But you sound different. Maybe it's because it's resolved.'

'What's resolved?'

'Your big issue. You and your crim have had your heart to heart and now you can move on from that. It's done more for you than you probably realise.'

I started to think she was right. I felt different from the way I had when I'd gone down to Sydney. Perhaps it had been the thing I needed before I could do this job properly.

***

I spoke to my parents on the phone and they were largely non-committal about the whole thing. I didn't understand why until late in the following day when I came back to Aunt Myrtle's place and my mother opened the door!

'What are you doing here?' I said, launching myself into her arms.

'Your dad and I thought that if you were unsure about whether or not to do this, the best way we could advise you is to see it for ourselves.'

I stepped out of her arms as my dad came to the door and I gave him a hug too. 'You didn't have to do that. Dad, you only just went back to Brisbane.'

'That was a few weeks ago now, in case you've forgotten,' he said with a laugh. 'And if you're going to work in a place like that, your mother wouldn't sleep at night if she hadn't checked it out first.'

Mum playfully swatted him. 'Don't be silly.'

But I knew he was serious. Things like this worried her. The trouble was, if she went to the church, she probably wouldn't feel much better, especially if she had an encounter with Angel.

***

I was nervous the following day when they came to the church with me. Pastor Matt welcomed them with open arms and was delighted when he heard why they had come.

'It's fantastic that you're so interested in your daughter's future work. Come and meet the kids.'

Matt didn't really need to say that because we were already in the auditorium and most of the kids were there and they'd heard what he'd said. They gazed almost disbelievingly at my parents. I guess the idea that parents cared enough to travel from Brisbane to Sydney just to check out their daughter's new workplace was hard for them to take in.

The boys were polite to them, although I could see them mentally cataloguing them as uncool. That didn't bother me. I'd done it myself often enough. However, Angel was a different matter.

She stood with arms folded before my mother, who gave her a tentative hello. Then Angel leant forward, hawking. I could see what she was about to do but knew I wouldn't get there in time to stop her.

Just when she was about to spit in Mum's face, Jacinta grabbed her and spun her around. 'Get out of here now,' she snapped.

Angel shrieked and swung her fists at her but Jacinta sidestepped and marched her out of the room with her arm behind her back while she screamed with rage.

I cleared my throat. 'That's Angel.'

'Really?' Mum said, clearly shaken.

Dad guided her to one of the chairs and I went and got them both cups of coffee. Most of the other kids went back to playing pool or whatever they had been doing before, all the while shooting curious looks at my parents. This increased when my father, downing the last of his coffee, jumped up and picked up a pool cue.

'I wanted to play last time I was here but I haven't played in a while,' he said to Brett. 'Can you cope with a beginner?'

Brett snorted. 'Whatever.'

I watched them as they played. My father was holding his own, which was good to see, although there was no doubt Brett had the upper hand. Not that that was a problem; my father could lose graciously. That was a skill that probably needed demonstrating.

My mother stirred her coffee thoughtfully. 'These children seem like quite the challenge.'

I looked around. Everyone else was behaving. Only Angel had caused a scene.

Mum looked at Bodin, who'd just come in with Alana. She shook her head. 'They could all do with a good role model.'

'They're not that bad, Mum.'

She frowned. 'I'm not talking about their behaviour, Madison.' She looked around the room again. 'It's that look in their eyes. They look like they don't care about anything.'

'Most of them are teenagers.'

'No, it's more than that.' Compassion filled her face.

I realised what she was seeing. A lot of the kids looked like they needed new clothes, but with that was something else—a look that said they had no expectations of anything. It was more than just teenage apathy. There was no hope.

I patted her hand. 'I know that, Mum. That's why they need help. Here we can help them realise that there's more to life than just struggling through things every day. It doesn't have to be like that. We're trying to help them understand that, to see beyond their circumstances.'

My mother gave me a small smile but said nothing.

I went back to watching Dad play pool. He had started playing against Jeremy and the others had gathered round to watch. I knew Jeremy was good and was surprised when he missed his first two shots.

My father was quick to take advantage of his mistakes. 'Looks like there's life in the old dog yet,' he said as he sank three balls in quick succession.

Jeremy took up his cue then and managed to sink a couple

before missing again. As my father stepped up to resume playing Jeremy glanced at me and winked. He'd never done that before and I could feel my face heating up. I felt Mum's eyes on me and turned back to her.

She gave Jeremy the once-over. 'And who's that boy?'

I didn't like her tone and decided honesty was the best way to kill what she was thinking. 'That's Jeremy Stannem. You know, the guy who held me up in the bookstore.'

Her eyes snapped back to him. 'Really?'

Once Dad had declared victory, they shook hands and my father came over to join us. Jeremy resumed playing with Brett. Dad's eyes narrowed as he watched his shots and I knew it didn't escape his notice how much better Jeremy was playing now he was out of the game.

'It seems I've been treated like the old man I am,' he said thoughtfully. Then he lowered his voice. 'That's the guy from the holdup, isn't it?'

I nodded.

His eyes turned back to Jeremy, studying him. 'Well, you'd never know it. He seems too controlled to do something like that.'

'I guess we're all capable of bad things sometimes, aren't we?'

He gave me a long look. 'That we are, darling. That we are. How do you feel about working with him?'

'It's not a problem.'

Both my parents studied me as I said that. I hoped they could see on my face that it was true.

The rest of the morning passed uneventfully. I was taking my parents elsewhere for lunch, so we said goodbye to the kids, Jeremy and Matt, and headed off.

We'd barely driven out of the car park when my dad spoke up. 'Well, Maddy, although I'm sure working there will be challenging for you, I can see you love it. And I think those kids could do with having someone like you around.'

Relief filled my heart. 'You think I should stay then?'

'If you're happy there, I think you can do a lot of good.'

I glanced at my mother. She was looking at her hands in her lap. 'What do you think, Mum?'

She sighed. 'I agree with your father. I won't say I'm happy about all those kids, but I'm sure you could help them. They need someone like you.'

'Mum, there are already good role models there.'

Her eyes darted in my direction. 'You're quick to leap to that boy's defence.'

I scowled. 'I wasn't just talking about Jeremy. There's Matt and Jacinta, the girl I'll be replacing, as well as others in the church who they see from time to time. And there's nothing wrong with Jeremy either. In fact, he's a great role model for the kids because he's been through the bad stuff and come out of it a decent human being.'

After that, the conversation drifted onto less controversial subjects but I was angry with Mum for assuming that it was impossible for me to work with Jeremy. I knew from what my dad had said earlier that he seemed to think it okay but it was clear my mother had her doubts.

I wished they could see what I could see. The Jeremy working at the church bore almost no resemblance to the guy who'd held me up in the bookstore. Now it was difficult to see him as anything other than who he was—a guy who was good at his job. I didn't think anyone would hesitate to work with him.

Chapter Eighteen

My parents only stayed for two days before driving back to Brisbane. My mother had wanted me to go with them but I'd refused.

Not that I would be far behind them. I needed to head back at the end of the week. Uni started again in ten days' time.

The week galloped towards a close. I barely had time to get all the information I needed from Jacinta about her responsibilities. I was going to try and come down during each holiday break while she was still working there.

'Don't worry,' she said, while I was looking frantic on my last day. 'I'll be here all year. We can phone and email and text.'

We were in the auditorium packing groceries. I could see the guys through the sliding glass doors. They were playing basketball with Jeremy. Angel was out there too, although she was sulking again. Bodin had caught her about to put glue in Alana's hair and had to be restrained from beating her senseless. She was lucky he was letting her stand there, especially since I could hear her abusive language loud and clear.

Alana was with us. She was helping to pack and seemed to be enjoying the girl time. 'It's gonna be so sad here when you go,' she lamented.

'Jacinta will still be here, you know.' I knew she would probably be more of a help with Angel than I was. She knew how to forcibly restrain her if she had to and I didn't know if I could do that.

'I know,' she said, throwing her arms around me. 'But you're just so ... nice.'

Nice. Yep, that was me in a nutshell. I wished she'd said I was a good counsellor or always knew the right thing to say or something that made me feel like I knew how to do this job.

I shook off those negative thoughts. Nice wasn't a bad thing.

Jacinta looked at the time. 'You need to get going, you know. You don't want to miss your flight.'

Alana pouted and I agreed with a sigh. 'I know. Just a few more boxes.'

She shook her head. 'No more boxes. You need to say goodbye to everyone and get going. I mean it.'

I knew she was right. 'Okay. Well, I hope I'll get to see you in a few months.' I gave Alana a hug and Jacinta a longer one. 'Thanks so much.'

'No worries. And don't you fret about the job.' She rubbed my arm. 'You'll do fine.'

I looked at the boys outside. I needed to say goodbye to them. It hurt just to think about it. I'd already said goodbye to Rory earlier that day. That had been almost impossible.

I heard Matt in the corridor outside and dashed out there to say goodbye to him first.

His eyes brightened as they saw me. 'You going now, are you? Well, at least I know it won't be long before we see you again.' He gave me a hug. 'Let us know when you get home safely, okay?'

'Sure thing.' I could feel tears gathering in my eyes. Who would have thought I'd be this emotional about leaving these people? The thought of meeting them had terrified me just weeks ago.

I went outside to where the guys were. Angel marched off in a huff as soon as she saw me coming. I guessed there would be no tears from her. The boys didn't seem to know whether to hug me or shake my hand. Bodin was the only one who pulled me into a hug before putting his hand on my butt.

'Watch it,' I growled.

He grinned as I stepped away and I knew he didn't mean anything by it. He was just trying to get a rise out of me.

'Bye, Hoop Girl,' said Brett, shaking my hand with a grin. That got all the boys saying it and I was still hearing chants of Hoop Girl as I turned to Jeremy.

I wasn't sure what to say or do. We stood there awkwardly for a minute before he held out his hand. 'I look forward to working with you.'

I'd wondered if he would give me a hug. I should have known that wasn't going to happen. He wouldn't initiate that kind of thing. So I shook his hand. 'Yeah. It should be great.'

Tears pricked my eyes as I turned and I blinked them back. I would see them all again in a few months. But that seemed like a long way away.

I headed around the corner to my car. I threw my bag inside, shut the door and leant on it. Everything in me was screaming.

Go back and see him, you idiot! Give him a hug. He's never going to think you forgive him if you leave like this!

I ran back towards the basketball court. As I reached the corner, I ran into Jeremy.

I stepped back, losing my balance, and he reached out and held my arms to steady me. We stood there like that for a moment, staring at one another.

'I'm sorry,' I said. 'I just wanted to say goodbye.'

Without waiting to see what he thought, I threw myself into his arms. As I felt his grip tighten around me, I didn't feel afraid.

He held me for longer than I would have expected. Then I heard his soft voice. 'Maddy, I'm so sorry.'

I stepped away and glared at him. 'You don't need to say that to me anymore. That's the past and you need to let it go.'

I could see the relief on his face, coupled with an almost reverent expression. 'Please know I'll never hurt you.'

'I know you won't. And I'll come back to prove it to you. You can count on it.' I grinned. 'Those kids won't know what hit them.'

He grinned back and followed me over to the car. He opened the door for me and shut it behind me, like he always did. Then he stepped back. 'Drive safe.'

I smiled. 'Don't worry. I'll be back here before you know it.'

Hesitation flashed in his eyes but it was soon replaced by resolution. 'I know you will.'

'Take care of Angel.'

He rolled his eyes. 'I'll try.'

'Okay. I'll see you soon.'

It felt strange leaving but I knew it was the right thing to do. I had a degree to finish. I had to tie up my life in Brisbane so I could move to Sydney.

The hug had been just as healing as the restoration conference. While Jeremy had done a terrible thing once, he regretted it and every part of him was now dedicated to repaying that debt and stopping others from making the same mistake.

I spared a thought for Evan but it was only brief. I truly hoped he'd find his way and learn to forgive himself for what had happened. Hopefully, he would get therapy and move on.

As for me, the only regret I had was leaving behind the kids, *my* kids. I knew the future I wanted and I knew where it was. I was sure the road I was taking wouldn't be a smooth one but I was stronger now. I could make a difference. I could help people. I'd make mistakes along the way, but it would work out.

And maybe bad things would happen again. I wasn't naïve enough to think they wouldn't. But I knew I could get through it, maybe with help, but I could make it. I might still become a victim, but I didn't have to stay a victim. I could rise above it.

He waved at me as I pulled out of the car park, heading off on the next part of my journey.